"I'm not much of a talker, but it doesn't mean that I don't listen or that I don't notice things."

"Such as?"

"The sky above us right now. You really should look up."

Cormac was right. The lights were in full spate now—mesmerizing pulses of emerald green shimmering and weaving through the sky like spirits playing chase. Time stretched away silently as they watched nature's extravagant spectacle, and for a moment, it felt to Milla that this heavenly light show was nature's gift to them both. Something to lift them out of themselves, if only for a short time. "It's beautiful, Cor, don't you think?"

"Amazing."

Something about the direction of his voice told her that he was no longer looking at the sky, and she turned to meet his gaze. The light shimmering from above threw luminous waves over his face so that she couldn't read the expression in his eyes or gauge his thoughts. "You *were* talking about the lights, weren't you?"

He hesitated briefly. "I was talking about the view."

Dear Reader,

I can't believe I'm writing this letter to introduce you to my debut novel for Harlequin. It's testimony to the fact that dreams really do come true.

I'm here because I won a writing competition, so I will always be grateful to Milla and Cormac for capturing the judges' hearts in that first chapter. Milla is inspired by a real person—an Irish art student—who I came across when she was modeling. I follow her blog, and it was her various residencies in the Outer Hebrides that gave me the idea that Milla should be an artist, seeking isolation in a remote Scottish bothy in order to heal her broken heart. I wanted Cormac to be more than the heir to Calcarron estate; I wanted him to be strong and physically capable, so giving him a career as a commander in the Royal Engineers ticked those boxes. His military life also gave me the perfect well from which to draw his traumatic backstory.

I love writing about Scotland and its people. I've tried to make my descriptive touches completely authentic, and while I use fragments of reality when I'm writing, I should point out that Calcarron Estate and its environs are completely fictitious.

I hope you enjoy reading this story as much as I enjoyed creating it.

Ella x

Her Brooding
Scottish Heir

—

Ella Hayes

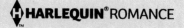

HARLEQUIN® ROMANCE

Recycling programs
for this product may
not exist in your area.

ISBN-13: 978-1-335-49921-9

Her Brooding Scottish Heir

First North American publication 2018

Copyright © 2018 by Ella Hayes

Printed in U.S.A.

After ten years as a television camerawoman, **Ella Hayes** started her own photography business so that she could work around the demands of her young family. As an award-winning wedding photographer, she's documented hundreds of love stories in beautiful locations, both at home and abroad. She lives in central Scotland with her husband and two grown-up sons. She loves reading, traveling with her camera, running and great coffee.

Her Brooding Scottish Heir
is Ella Hayes's debut title for Harlequin!

Visit the Author Profile page at Harlequin.com.

For Sophie

CHAPTER ONE

MILLA O'BRIEN GLANCED at the map open on the passenger seat. She'd circled landmarks with a pink highlighter so she'd be able to track her progress north, and now that she'd passed the last pink circle—a stone bridge over sparkling amber water—she knew that she was only fifteen miles from the Calcarron Estate. In front of her the narrow road snaked through the glen, a grey ribbon rippling through a perfect wilderness.

It was a wilderness she longed for. London held too many memories, too much heartbreak. It was impossible to work there now. She needed a clean slate. These two weeks of perfect isolation at Strathburn Bothy would give her some time to heal; give her a chance to get back on track with her portfolio. Her postgraduate art exhibition was six weeks away and she was seriously behind schedule.

The road ahead straightened and she accelerated, stretching her eyes to the immensity of the landscape. The glinting May sunshine lured subtle hues from the surly mountains while the wind played with tufts of yellow grass on the lower slopes. The beauty and freedom of the scene bolstered her spirits—and then suddenly the steering wheel shifted in her hands as the four-by-four lurched to the right.

The ominous clopping sound coming from the back told her all she needed to know. She stopped and pulled on the handbrake. Perfect. Miles from anywhere and she'd got a puncture.

She jumped down from the driver's seat and inspected the deflated rear tyre. At least she wasn't completely clueless. A mechanic father and three petrol-head brothers had given her a working knowledge of car maintenance, if only by osmosis.

She found the jack and wheel brace behind the driver's seat, then hefted the spare wheel off the back. She knew about loosening the nuts on the flat wheel before jacking up the car, so she slotted the wheel spanner over a nut and worked her weight against it.

It wouldn't give.

She tried again, to no avail, so she stood on the spanner and bounced up and down, but it still wouldn't budge. She tried a different nut, then each nut in turn. The damned things were immovable.

Confounded, she plonked herself down on the rear bumper to catch her breath. She'd have to call for help, assuming she could even get a signal.

She'd just retrieved her phone from the door pocket when the distant sound of an approaching car caught her attention. Shielding her eyes from the sun, she watched as a silver sports car flew down the straight towards her. The car slowed as it drew nearer, and then it pulled over.

Milla felt her heart begin to thump. It was an isolated spot and she was a girl on her own. She glanced at her phone—no signal.

The car door swung open and she stepped back as a pair of light hazel eyes pinned her with an appraising stare. The driver didn't smile. Instead, he looked at her as if she was an irritating problem he'd have to solve, but his gaze held no threat. He'd clearly stopped to help her, even if he intended to do so with very little grace.

He slid out of his seat and walked towards her, his eyes darting to the flat tyre and abandoned wheel brace. 'You look like you know what you're doing, and I'm not trying to step on your toes, but I thought I should stop to see if you need any help.'

He might be in his late twenties, but he

seemed to lack the exuberance of youth. Milla couldn't decide if he was bad-tempered or desperately sad.

She motioned to the wheel. 'I do know what I'm doing, but I can't actually do it. Those damn air ratchets over-tighten the nuts so you need superhuman strength to loosen them. And there's no leverage on that short wheel brace, so, yes, please, I do need some help, if you don't mind.'

His eyes seemed to register faint amusement, but before she could be sure he was striding towards the listing vehicle. He rolled up his shirt-sleeves and crouched down to the wheel. He slotted the wheel spanner over the lowest nut and pushed his weight against it.

His brown hair was close-cropped, and his muscular forearms were tanned, but Milla sensed that it was colour earned from outdoor work. He looked like an outdoor type, strong and capable. When he glanced up at her she felt herself unravelling just a little bit.

'They *are* tight—'

'Just like I said they were.' The words flew from her mouth before she could stop them. She was horrified. What had got into her?

He pushed harder and the spanner shifted. He worked the nut loose and moved on to the next one. When he spoke again, he didn't look up. 'You're Irish.'

'You're observant.'

Why couldn't she couldn't switch off this compulsion to goad him? She felt a frown creasing her forehead. Maybe she'd turned into one of those women who blame all men for the transgressions of one. She sighed. If he'd smiled, introduced himself, acted like a normal person, maybe she'd be acting differently too.

When he'd loosened all the nuts he reached for the jack. 'Would you like me to finish the job?'

She couldn't fathom his thoughts. His eyes were filled only with the question he'd asked and yet her heart was racing. She didn't trust herself to speak again so she just smiled and nodded.

With practised expertise he changed the wheel, lowered the jack and tightened the nuts. 'I'll put the flat wheel in the back. There's a mechanic in Ardoig who'll fix it for you.'

She opened the rear door and he thumped the wheel down. If he'd noticed her easel and canvases he chose not to comment. He pushed the door closed and turned to face her. 'Be sure to have that fixed.'

'Yes, sir.'

She saw his eyes cloud and instantly regretted her teasing. She attempted to warm him with a smile.

'Seriously, thanks very much. It was lucky for me that you were passing.' She shrugged. 'There's no signal here so I couldn't have called for help. You've saved me a very long walk and at least three fingernails.'

He placed the wheel brace into her hands, the ghost of a smile on his lips. 'It *was* lucky. I very rarely come this way.'

He nodded slightly, then turned back to his car. In a moment he'd started the engine and disappeared, leaving Milla in a cloud of dust.

As he accelerated away Cormac Buchanan let his eyes linger on the girl in his rear-view mirror. When he couldn't see her any more he conjured the memory of her dancing green eyes as she'd teased him. Perhaps he'd deserved it. Five years in the Royal Engineers, ordering the sappers about, had undoubtedly affected his manner. Still, she hadn't been fazed and he admired her spirit.

A rare light-heartedness seized him as he took the next bend. Who was he trying to fool? It wasn't only her spirit he'd admired. He'd also admired her smile, her milky skin and the blonde hair tumbling out of the clip she'd been wearing.

Even if he hadn't seen the easel and canvases in the back of her vehicle he'd have guessed that she was some kind of artist. Those tight-fitting red jeans tucked into green Doc Marten boots, the ripped denim waistcoat over a battered vest and the studs climbing halfway up her left ear had spoken of an expressive personality. He imagined that her painting would be bold, a little edgy, and there'd be a small quirk in it somewhere, something to remind the viewer not to take it all too seriously.

What was he doing? Ten minutes with the pretty Irish artist and she'd got him painting his own scenarios. He needed to focus on the road and get to Calcarron before his sister, Rosie, had another pre-wedding meltdown.

It was only a week until Rosie's big day, and he'd already had his fill of emails about the endless list of things she needed him to do. An interior designer by profession, Rosie had big plans for her wedding at the family home. She'd reasoned that since her guests were travelling such a long way, she wanted to create something spectacular for them.

His own view was that the wedding itself should be the main attraction, but he knew from experience that once Rosie had made up her mind about something the best policy was to fall in with her. She'd asked him to oversee the positioning and erection of the marquee, the dance floor and the miles of suspended lighting she wanted in the trees and along the pathways. There were umpteen jobs to do, all of which, she had flattered him by saying, required military precision.

He stopped for a ewe that had wandered onto the road with her twin lambs. She regarded him with a wary maternal eye then moved on, the lambs tripping after her on spindly legs. He sighed. He would do anything for Rosie, but being back at Calcarron under the watchful eye of his family was going to be hard.

Afghanistan had changed him. His friend's death had changed him. He couldn't seem to get past it and coming back was only going to feed the ache of his loss because his memories of Duncan were inextricably meshed with his memories of home.

He couldn't feel excited about the wedding, not even for his sister, and the thought of making small talk with two hundred guests on the wedding day itself was filling him with dread. There were expectations associated with being the Laird's son and heir, and Cormac felt the weight of those expectations like a millstone around his neck.

The only way he'd survive the coming week would be by keeping his head down. He imagined Rosie frowning at him for such morose thoughts, but as long as he kept them to himself and got on with things maybe he'd get through somehow, and manage not to upset anyone.

Milla sat for a few moments and considered the hazel-eyed stranger who'd stopped to help her. How had he got under her skin so quickly? He'd made her nervous; she always ran off at the mouth when she was nervous. She plucked at a loose thread on the hem of her vest. She'd been defensive from the start—prickly and defensive—and it wasn't her real nature at all.

It was Dan's fault. He was responsible for making her feel so hostile, so wary, so utterly diminished. If this was the legacy of love, she wanted no part of it ever again.

She turned the key in the ignition, but instead of driving away she stared through the windscreen in a kind of trance. Such sad eyes... If only he'd smiled he'd have looked quite handsome. A bit of small talk would have made a difference, something other than the distinctly unimaginative *'You're Irish'.*

What was she supposed to do with that? She winced, remembering her reply. What had got into her? No wonder he'd focussed on changing the wheel.

She squeezed her eyes shut and tried to shake the confusion out of her head. Maybe he'd have liked her better if she'd played the damsel in distress, but that wasn't her style. She wasn't interested in flattering any man's vanity.

She pulled away and quickly shifted through the gears. What did it matter if he liked her or not anyway? He was gone, and she needed to find the garage in Ardoig.

When she reached the village it wasn't difficult to spot the garage because, apart from a tiny supermarket and an ancient-looking hotel, that was all there was. A ruddy-faced man with a salt-and-pepper beard said he could fix the puncture while she waited, and since she needed to buy a few provisions anyway she ventured over to the shop.

Inside, the air was rich with the mingling aromas of fresh bread, detergent and mothballs. She patrolled the narrow aisles, filling a basket with a few essentials, and was deliberating over the bread rolls when a woman came in.

'Hello, Mary. That's me in for my lottery ticket.'

'Right you are, Sheila. Lucky Dip?'

'Aye, go on, then. Did you see Cormac's car go past? He's back for the wedding anyway.'

'Aye. He'll be busy. Rosie's got grand schemes, apparently.'

Milla wondered if she should get some candles. There was electricity at the bothy, but it wouldn't hurt to be prepared. She located tea lights and a box of matches, then approached the till and perused the magazine covers while the lottery ticket transaction was being concluded.

The two women weren't in a hurry, in fact, they didn't seem to have noticed her.

'Jessie says she thinks he's still not right, you know. Such a shame.'

Milla noticed a rack of Ordnance Survey maps and reached one down. With no phone signal where she was going, she wouldn't be able to use an app when she was out walking. A map would be useful; she didn't want to get lost.

'Ach, well, he'll have to move on sooner or later. You can't carry that stuff around with you for ever... Sorry, love, I didnae see you there. I'll be with you in a moment.'

Milla smiled and switched her basket to the other hand.

'Anyway, Rosie's going to be a beautiful bride. She's here already, with her bridesmaids. Lily says they're making all the wedding favours themselves.' The machine spat out a square of pink paper. 'Okay, here's your winning ticket.'

Mary winked at her friend and Sheila chuckled.

'Aye, that'd be right. See you later.'

Sheila disappeared through the door with a backwards wave.

Mary smiled. 'Sorry for keeping you, dear.' She scanned Milla's items through the till, her fingers lingering on the map. 'Are you a walker?'

Milla smiled. 'No, well, sort of... I'm an artist—'

'Ah, you'll be staying up at Strathburn, then?'

Milla nodded. 'I need peace and quiet to work on my exhibition folio.'

Mary raised her eyebrows as she stowed Milla's shopping into a bag. 'Well, you might have picked the wrong week. There's a wedding at the big house on Saturday, so we're going to be mobbed. Do you know your way up to the bothy from here?'

'A wedding—' Milla swallowed the lump in her throat and managed a smile. 'How lovely. I've got directions for Strathburn... Through the village, next right towards Calcarron, then left up a track...?'

'Aye...up the track for about a mile and a half. If you like, I'll phone the manager and tell him you're on your way—then he can meet you there with the key.'

She felt warmed by Mary's kindness. This community spirit reminded her of her home in Ireland. 'That'd be grand, thank you. I'm just

getting a puncture fixed at the garage and then
I'll be on my way.'

'Right you are. I'll tell him. See you later.'

At the gates to Calcarron House Cormac
stopped and let the car idle. He closed his eyes,
reminded himself that it was Rosie's wedding—
she was going to be the centre of attention. With
a big wedding to gossip about, it should be easy
for him to pass under the radar, but this was a
small community.

Everyone knew he was struggling to come to
terms with Duncan's death—even his mother
had used the phrase 'PTSD' once—but he knew
it wasn't that. He'd simply been shredded by
grief and he didn't know how to put himself back
together; he couldn't make sense of the world
any more, or understand his place within it.

At the barracks it was easier—he was just another emotional casualty—but here he'd have to
weather the curious looks, tactfully deflect the
subtly loaded questions and, for Rosie's sake,
he'd have to pretend that he was absolutely fine.

He drew a breath and slid the car through
the gates.

At the sight of the house he felt a momentary joy. He'd almost forgotten how much he
loved Calcarron, with its turreted gables and
mullioned windows, and as he lifted his bag

from the back seat he smiled at the muffled swell of barking he could hear coming from inside. When the front door opened, the baying split the air and three ecstatic Labradors bounded towards him, followed by the slender figure of his mother.

'Tyler, Mungo, Crash— Whoa, calm down!'

The dogs tangled into his legs, butting their wet noses and tongues into his hands. He stroked their sleek black coats, rubbed the broad, noble heads, laughing in spite of himself at such uncomplicated affection.

'Cormac!' Lily Buchanan wrapped her arms around him, then stood back and studied his face. 'I'm so glad you're here. Everyone's a little giddy and I'm going quite mad with it all. I could use an ally.'

He gave her a knowing look. 'It's only Rosie's wedding. It'll be a walk in the park.'

She grimaced as he picked up his bag and threw an arm around her shoulders.

'"A walk in the park" is not the expression I would have chosen, but anyway, let's go inside. Rosie and the girls are dying to see you, and I warn you, she's got a wedding spreadsheet on her laptop.'

In the drawing room Rosie and her three bridesmaids were discussing the décor for the marquee. With the introductions over, Cormac sank into an armchair and listened half-heartedly. He loved this room, with its high ceilings and over-stuffed sofas, its shelves lined with books and family photos in silver frames. Over the fire-place hung an oil painting of a magnificent stag; perhaps it wasn't quite as fine as Landseer's *Monarch of the Glen* but he admired it even so. Like everything else at Calcarron, it was freighted with a lifetime's worth of memories.

In spite of his misgivings, it felt good to be back. The estate was in his blood and would be-long to him one day—sooner rather than later if his father had anything to do with it. He wanted to go for a walk, get acclimatised after his long drive, but it wouldn't be polite to disappear so soon after arriving.

'Cor!'

He heard his name and looked up.

'So, while you do all the outside stuff,' Rosie was saying, 'we're going to do all the finishing touches—it's a woodland theme, with foraged greenery, and we're using jam jars with strips of tartan ribbon and hessian to make tea light holders for the tables…'

Cormac felt his attention wandering. It wasn't that he didn't want Rosie to have her dream wedding—he was here to help after all—he just couldn't get excited about woodland themes and tea lights while people were dying in wars.

Rosie was trying to create a Scottish *themed* wedding. Wasn't the place itself enough? Why did she want to underline everything with tartan? Perhaps his mother had been right—they were all giddy with wedding planning. The sooner he could get on with his list of outside jobs the better. He certainly wouldn't be able to fake interest in this kind of minutiae for a whole week.

He wondered how his brother, Sam, was coping with it all. Happy-go-lucky Sam, who was notably absent. Perhaps that was the trick.

Lily swung through the door with a loaded tea tray and Cormac got up to carry it for her. As he set the tray down on the coffee table Rosie caught his eye, sprang to her feet and pulled him into a hug.

'Thanks for coming to help with the wedding. I really appreciate it.' She leaned in to his ear and whispered. 'I'm so preoccupied—I haven't even asked you how you *are*.' She squeezed his hand. 'We'll chat later, okay?'

With the tea poured, Cormac lifted a cup from the tray and retreated to the relative seclusion of the bay window, where he gazed out over the view he loved.

The well-tended garden descended gently to

the edges of the loch. Loch Calcarron was the jewel in the crown of the family estate, flanked by steeply climbing slopes with purple mountains beyond.

'Where's Sam?' he asked.

Rosie was handing round shortbread. 'He was up at the bothy this morning, getting things ready for the artist who's arriving today, and then he went fishing. Can you see his boat out there?'

At the mention of a new artist at the bothy Cormac felt a rush of something indefinable attached to a memory of teasing green eyes.

He forced himself to focus on the expanse of loch in front of him. 'I can't see his boat. Maybe he capsized…' As he suspected, no one was listening to him.

He heard one of the girls ask what a bothy was, and Lily's voice rising in explanation.

'Traditional bothies are small stone structures where walkers can shelter or stay overnight, but what we have is an artist's bothy. Rosie's grandfather was a keen amateur artist. When artists' bothies started springing up in remote places he thought it was a wonderful idea. Calcarron Estate is large. We have plenty of space. So he said we should build one too—let artists come to enjoy all the things we take for granted. We hired an architect to design something practical and comfortable and we located it right up in the hills. Splendid isolation and all that. It's very popular.'

Rosie interjected. 'It's a large wooden hut basically, but a contemporary design. There's a deck in front, overlooking the hills, and this year Sam's installed one of those big hammocks, so guests can chill out with the amazing view, or even watch the stars at night. The living space is bright and airy because of the picture windows, and we designed the studio with opaque roof panels, so it's got perfect light for working. There's a cute wood stove, which keeps the place cosy when it's cold, but my very favourite part is the mezzanine bedroom—it's so romantic. I did the interior design—I can show you some photogra—'

Lily held up her hand. 'Is that the telephone…?'

Cormac seized the opportunity. 'I'll go.'

His mother's voice faded as he escaped to the kitchen and hooked the receiver off the phone on the wall. 'Buchanan.'

'Is that you, Sam?' The female voice sounded hesitant.

'No, it's Cormac—'

'Cormac! It's Mary Frazer, from the shop in Ardoig. How are you?'

He wasn't good at small talk, but since the

local shop was Gossip Central it was impera-
tive that he sounded politely upbeat. 'Ah, hello,
Mary. I'm fine, thanks. What can I do for you?'

'I've had your bothy guest in the shop just
now and I said I'd call to let you know she's on
her way, so you can meet her there with the key.
Sam usually—'

'Thanks, Mary. I'll send him.'

'Well, you might wait a while, mind. She said
she was having a wheel fixed, or something, before she comes up...'

Cormac felt his heart tightening in his chest
and he swallowed hard. 'Okay, thanks for letting us know. Bye for now.'

He didn't mean to hurry Mary off the phone,
but he had the impression she'd have talked
on and on and he simply couldn't. He leaned
against the wall and tipped back his head. So
the artist with the puncture was their new bothy
guest. He didn't understand why the news had
caused his pulse to spike. She was striking, of
course, and rather abrasive, but there was something else too, hidden in her eyes...vulnerabil-
ity, perhaps?

Suddenly Lily appeared through the door.
'Are you all right, Cor?'

He shook himself and met her gaze. 'I'm fine.
Just tired from the drive, I suppose, and all that

wedding chat… You weren't wrong. It's going to be quite a week.'

Lily patted his arm. 'It'll be fine. Once Dad's home you can hide in his study, drink whisky and talk about estate business. Who was that on the telephone?'

'It was Mary, from the shop. She was calling to say that the new incumbent is on her way up to the bothy.'

Lily frowned. 'Damn your brother. The bothy and its guests are supposed to be his responsibility. He's taking advantage, of course. *Cormac's coming home so I'll go fishing and let him take over.*'

'Me?'

'Would you mind?' Lily shot him a sly smile. 'It means you can escape the clutches of Bridezilla and her handmaidens and you can take the new quad bike. A ride up the hill will soon blow away the cobwebs.' She opened the dresser drawer and handed him a stag's horn key fob. 'It doesn't take long to do the show-around and go over a few safety points. By the time you get back we'll be ready for pre-dinner drinks.'

Cormac pocketed the key. He could hardly refuse, since Sam was AOL, and hadn't he just been thinking about getting out for a walk? If he could deal with the bothy business quickly he'd have time to go up to the ridge before dinner. It was his favourite place, and the perfect antidote to wedding fever.

He moved towards the door.

'Hang on.' Lily was leafing through a large blue book. 'Our new artist is called Camilla O'Brien.' She looked into his face and smiled. 'What a lovely name. You never know, Cor, she might be young and pretty.'

With her puncture fixed, Milla left Ardoig. The directions she'd been sent were clear enough, and she soon found the gate to the rough road she was to follow. At first the track wound through deciduous woodland, but soon she was out of the trees and heading steeply upwards.

The ride became bumpier, banks of loose gravel and the occasional pothole suggesting that water gushed down here in torrents when the rain was heavy. In low gear, she pressed on, climbing higher and higher, an edginess about the unfamiliar route causing her to chew at her bottom lip.

She reminded herself that first journeys always felt strange. Once she knew the way it would feel different.

After jolting up the track for what seemed like an eternity, the terrain levelled and she found herself crossing wild heathland towards another short ascent. From the top, she caught her first glimpse of the bothy, nestling against a steep hill. She stopped the vehicle and gazed down on it in delight.

It reminded her of a gypsy caravan without wheels, except that it was much larger. It had a tin roof with a round chimney, and in front she could see a broad deck with what looked like a hammock suspended on a giant wooden frame. With a happy sigh she rolled on and completed the final bumping descent to her new home.

She killed the engine and burst from the cab. After the sheer magnificence of the view, and the pleasing architecture of the bothy itself, the first thing she noticed was the silence. It was almost deafening. For a moment she forgot the heartache that had brought her here and stepped onto the deck, stretched her arms wide and twirled a slow, happy circle. This place was perfect.

She tried the door, just in case, but it was locked, so she pressed her nose to the glass and peered inside. The décor was simple. Bleached wooden floors, a grey linen sofa softened by a moss-green mohair blanket draped over one of its arms. A small black stove squatted in the corner of the main living area, and if she squinted sideways and looked up she could see a narrow wooden staircase leading to the mezzanine sleeping area. It was achingly romantic.

She felt a familiar stab of anguish and turned

away. On the hammock, she sank backwards, giving herself up to the gentle sway and creak of the canvas. She lifted her left hand, traced the outline of the absent ring with her right index finger.

She'd had her whole future mapped out before Dan had delivered his *coup de grâce*. She'd been planning their wedding when he'd flown over from Berlin to tell her that he'd fallen in love with Maria. He said it had just happened, that it wasn't his fault. Then he'd gone back to Germany and she'd been left to cancel everything.

Phone calls to suppliers. Phone calls to her family in Ireland.

She knew her father had tried to sound disappointed for her sake, but she had been able to picture the relief on his face. He'd never liked Dan. Neither had her brothers. She'd never felt so alone in her life. How desperately she'd needed her mother then, but her mother wasn't here any more, so she'd had to cope—whatever that meant.

She'd come to Strathburn to escape and to heal, to find some tiny piece of herself she could nurture back to life. If she could get back on track with her work, if she could properly lose herself in it, then maybe the world would start to make sense again.

The sound of an engine thrumming somewhere lower down the slope jerked her out of her melancholy. She levered herself off the hammock, crossed the deck and ran across the track to a vantage point overlooking the hill. Her eyes narrowed as she watched a vaguely familiar figure pounding a quad bike up the slope towards her, and then her breath caught in her throat as she realised, unequivocally, that the man riding towards her was the man who'd changed her wheel.

CHAPTER TWO

As HE PULLED the quad onto the track Milla caught herself fidgeting with the hem of her vest and stilled her hands before he could notice. She didn't understand why he made her nervous, other than that he seemed so...unreachable.

To make up for her prickly behaviour at the roadside, she'd smiled and given him a wave as he'd driven up the slope towards her, but he'd seemed intent on the business of navigating the quad through the heather and hadn't noticed her, so she'd felt foolish and, inexplicably, a little hurt.

As she waited for him to park and switch off the engine she told herself she was being overly sensitive, too ready to find rejection where none was intended. She drew in a breath, resolving to be open and friendly.

'Hello again.' She took a step towards him. 'We keep meeting in remote places. Should I be worried that you're stalking me?'

He looked up, the ghost of a smile on his lips. 'It's purely coincidental, I promise. You must be Camilla O'Brien.'

'Must I?' She smiled. 'My name's Milla—Camilla's a bit too "jolly hockey sticks" for my liking.'

She was gratified to see his cheeks creasing into a smile as he swung off the quad, but when he looked up again it had disappeared.

'Okay, Milla. I've got your key.'

The smile he'd tried to conceal had transformed his face into something beautiful, and for some reason she wanted to see it again.

She looked at him expectantly, and when he met her gaze blankly she lifted her eyebrows. 'Do you also have a name?'

He pressed the heel of his hand against his forehead. 'I'm sorry—it's been a long day.' He held out his hand. 'I'm Cormac Buchanan.'

'It's nice to meet you, Cormac—officially this time.' She stretched her hand to his.

For a dizzy moment she lost herself in the golden light of his irises. She felt the warm dryness of his palm against hers, a pinprick of static. She released his hand quickly.

'Buchanan? You're the owner of the estate?'

He shook his head. 'One day, maybe. For now I'm running errands.'

She couldn't resist a little mischief. 'Well, I

suppose it's like any job. You have to start at the bottom and work up.'

A smile seemed to tug at the corners of his mouth and then it faded away. She felt her brow wrinkling. Did Cormac Buchanan not have a sense of humour? Maybe she was being too familiar, overstepping some invisible mark unique to estate owners. She couldn't work out what she was doing wrong.

She was about to ask him if she could just have the key, when she saw his gaze shifting to the four-by-four.

'I see you got your wheel fixed.'

'Yes, the man at the garage was able to do it right away.'

'That's good.' He glanced at her and reached into his pocket. 'Right. I'll open up and help you in with your stuff, then I'll show you the ropes.'

He pulled out a key and motioned for her to walk with him to the bothy door.

Milla frowned as she fell in beside him. She could never have accused Cormac Buchanan of being impolite, but she had the distinct feeling that he was keeping her at arm's length, and for some reason it felt like a personal slight.

She caught herself shifting into that defensive gear which seemed to have become her default setting since Dan had dropped his bombshell, and she only just managed to keep a sliver of sarcasm out of her voice. 'Thanks, but I wouldn't want to put you to any trouble.'

He unlocked the bothy door and stood back for her to enter. 'It's no trouble at all. It's why I'm here.'

Milla stepped past him into the bothy and instantly her mood lifted. The interior space felt warm and comfortable and completely connected to the outside. It wasn't just that the floor-to-ceiling windows let the outside in; the colours and textures of the interior had also clearly been chosen to echo the view.

This sanctuary was to be her home for the next two weeks and already she felt its gentle embrace soothing her shrunken soul.

For a moment she dropped her guard and turned around, smiling. 'It's stunning. Absolutely perfect. It's been so well done—I can't believe it—these colours and the textures—it's just... Wow!'

His expression softened, and for a moment he looked hesitant. 'My sister's an interior designer. She's good. She did the whole place—natural materials to blend with the setting.'

There was obvious pride in his voice. It was clear that his sister meant a lot to him and the small revelation made him seem more approachable.

Milla's eyes followed his as they roamed around the room.

'This is the main living area, obviously. Have you used a wood burner before?'

'Yes, I have. We had one at home.'

She turned and crossed to the compact stove with its gleaming glass door. It looked state-of-the-art, not like her family's old stove. She tried the handle, pulling it open while he continued speaking.

'There's a log store against the outside wall of the bothy, and it's well stocked, so if you feel cold just set a fire. You'll find firelighters and matches in that metal box on the hearth. It doesn't take long to heat the whole place.'

Without the distraction of his face, she tuned in to the husky timbre of his voice and found a gentleness in it which took her by surprise. She closed the stove and stood up.

'As you can see, the kitchen's over there—it's well equipped as far as it goes. There's all the usual stuff. The plates and cups are in the cupboards over the counter. I'm afraid there isn't a dishwasher—'

His earnest tone made her laugh. 'I don't mind washing dishes—but there won't be many. I don't really cook much when I'm working. I tend to forget and then I'll eat a whole stupid box of cornflakes or something.'

Did she imagine amusement in his eyes or was it disdain? She looked away quickly, flushing with embarrassment. What had possessed her to come out with that anyway? Nerves, most probably—that must be it—from the way he seemed to take up all the space in the room just by standing there.

'The bathroom's down that short corridor. It's a shower, not a bath, but you probably guessed that already, and the bedroom's up there...'

She looked up to the mezzanine, then turned to meet his gaze. 'I know—' She was blushing again. 'What I mean is that I saw it through the window before you arrived.' Why did his eyes unsettle her so much?

She forced herself to look away, to find a distraction.

'What a great idea to frame an Ordnance Survey map! I just bought one in the shop. If only I'd known there was one on the wall—'

She heard him clear his throat. 'The studio's through the door under the stairs, if you want to have a look. I'll start bringing in your things.'

He nodded briefly, then disappeared through the door.

Milla squeezed her eyes shut and blew out a long breath. She knew she'd been talking nonsense about the map, but she'd only been trying to fill the silence between them, and now, yet again, she was sparring with herself, trying to convince herself that he hadn't interrupted her to cause offence. It was understandable that he'd want to unload her vehicle and finish showing her 'the ropes', as he'd put it, but his cool detachment had hurt her all the same. He might be a laird-in-waiting, or whatever it was called, but he really needed to work on his social skills.

She forced Cormac Buchanan out of her head and focused on her surroundings. In the kitchen a wide timber plank had been repurposed as a counter, and she trailed her fingers along it, letting its smoothness steady her until she suddenly remembered that she was supposed to be looking at the studio.

When she pushed open the door she gasped. The studio was bigger than she'd imagined— as large again as the main living area. Daylight flooded in through the opaque roof panels and the resulting light had a luminous quality which was perfect.

When Cormac appeared with her easel and an armful of blank canvases, she couldn't contain her enthusiasm. 'I love this space. The light's exquisite.'

He propped the easel and canvases against the wall and turned around. 'Yes. It's been well thought out.' He ran a hand through his hair. 'Most of your stuff's in now. I put your holdall upstairs. There's just a couple of boxes left to bring.'

For a moment, he held her in his gaze, and she felt a strange shifting sensation beneath her feet, and then he was gone. She wondered if he'd been about to say something, then decided it was probably her overactive imagination. He wasn't much for talking.

She tucked a lock of hair behind her ear and looked around again. Such lovely light, such tranquillity. She felt a smile lifting the corners of her mouth. She didn't know if it was inspiration she was feeling, or simple happiness at being in such a wonderful place, but suddenly all she wanted was to be alone, to settle herself in and make the bothy feel like her own.

If she could wrap things up with Cormac quickly, she could start enjoying the solitude she'd come here for.

She was stowing milk and yoghurts in the tiny fridge when she heard him set down the last two boxes.

'That's everything. Before I go, I need to take you through one or two things...'

She wondered how she could tell him that she needed to be on her own. Would he understand that she was tired from her journey? Would he understand that his cool manner was making her feel even more inconsequential than she felt already?

She took a deep breath and stood up. 'Look, I appreciate your time and everything, but I'm happy to take it from here. I'm sure you must have other more important things…'

He recoiled slightly. 'I need to go through some safety—'

'No, honestly. It's fine. There's a book here.' She picked up the welcome pack she'd found near the kettle, holding it up for him to see. 'Look—*Strathburn Bothy: Essential Information*—I'll see if there's anything about safety.'

She flicked through the pages with a pounding heart. She could feel the weight of his stare, sense some indefinable emotion, but there was no going back now. She wasn't trying to challenge him; she just wanted to be at peace in her own space.

She found the page and opened it out to show him. 'It's all here, see: Safety Procedures. I'm sure it's got everything I need to know.' She looked into his face, noted the bruised look in his eyes and relented a little. 'Look, I promise I'll read it, okay? You can test me on it if it makes you feel better.'

She noticed the tiny flinch of a muscle in his jaw as he stepped towards her and handed her the key. 'As long as you read it, then—it is important. I hope you have a good stay, Milla.'

He held her gaze for moment, then nodded briefly and strode out of the door.

She sagged against the counter with relief. She could tell from his eyes that she'd offended him somehow, but when she replayed their conversation in her head, she couldn't see how. She'd been perfectly polite. In fact, she'd been exactly like him.

She looked down at her hands, saw that her fingers were trembling. When had dealing with men become so difficult? There always seemed to be an emotional price to pay.

She picked up the kettle, jiggled off the lid and reached for the tap. This break at Strathburn was exactly what she needed. Until she could cope with herself again she had no hope of dealing with anyone else.

Cormac jumped onto the quad, but didn't start the engine. Instead, he let his eyes travel over the landscape while he tried to pinpoint exactly how a simple mission to show someone around what was essentially a hut could have failed so miserably. She'd sent him packing, and even now the memory of those challenging eyes was making him wince.

He couldn't work her out. She was either teasing him or scowling at him, so he had no idea which way to jump. She was perplexing, but at the same time, she was refreshingly forthright. The memory of her mischievous smile, that defiant little tilt of her chin as she'd corrected him about her name, forced a brief smile onto his own lips.

He pictured the curve of her cheek, those tiny freckles on her nose. The way the sun's slanting rays had made her eyes shine. How delighted she'd been with the bothy—as if he'd opened a door for her straight into happiness. When she'd crouched to look at the wood burner he'd caught himself crossing a line—admiring the way her jeans moulded to her slender thighs, the way her waist nipped in, the rise of her breasts beneath the vest and waistcoat.

It had been a long time since he'd noticed anyone—*really* noticed anyone—and it felt like a little wrench inside. He was so used to the huge pain of losing his friend that most of the time he was numb, but this girl, the way she'd looked in the soft light of the studio, with her hair falling around her face and those eyes holding him… It had felt as if she could see right inside him, and he'd wanted to say something, but he hadn't because he hadn't known what it was he wanted to say.

Through the trees at the bottom of the hill,

he could see the turreted gables of Calcarron House and he imagined his father in the study, pouring a dram to welcome him home. In the drawing room the girls would be sipping tall gin and tonics, with thick slices of lemon, and his mother would be checking her watch, wondering where he was.

He turned the key in the ignition. They were waiting for him, but he couldn't go back right away. He wanted to go to the ridge, spend time with his memories…

'Cor—mac!'

He heard his name being called and turned to see Milla running along the track towards him. He killed the engine, tried to read her expression as she drew near.

She slowed, then stopped, her voice a little breathless from running. 'I'm so glad I caught you…!' She was twisting delicate fingers into the hem of her vest. 'There's no water coming out of the tap. I was going to make a cup of tea, but there's nothing. And no water from the bathroom taps either. Do you think you can fix it?'

He saw a glimmer of fragility in her eyes and sighed. 'Honestly—I don't know.' He swung off the quad and tried to sound optimistic. 'I'll take a look and see what I can do.'

She looked grateful and he hoped her gratitude would be justified. In the Royal Engineers, water systems had been his speciality. He was adept at sinking boreholes and building waste water treatment systems, but he'd found that nothing could be trickier than tracing a fault in a domestic water system—especially this kind of system. He certainly wasn't going to tell her that amphibians were a regular cause of blockages.

Inside the bothy, she hung back, shrugged an apology. 'I'd offer you a cup of tea, but…'

Her incessant mischief amused him, but he couldn't let it show. Since Duncan died, fun had become a luxury he couldn't afford, so he just nodded and went to check the filters.

Sam changed the filters regularly, so it was no surprise to find that they were clean, but the water level in the canisters was low, which meant that the problem had to be somewhere between the tank and the bothy.

The tank was located up the hill and the pipe to the bothy was partially buried. It might take hours to find the problem, and with evening already advancing there were literally not enough hours left in the day. It would have to wait until tomorrow.

There was no question of letting Milla stay in the bothy without a water supply. She'd have to spend the night at Calcarron. It was the only solution he could offer.

* * *

'You mean I'll have to stay at Calcarron House?'

The disappointment he'd seen in her eyes haunted him as he nosed the quad down the hillside through clumps of flowering heather. He realised that staying at the house wasn't exactly what she'd planned, but her reaction had seemed disproportionate to the inconvenience. Shooting parties paid a fortune to stay at Calcarron; surely she could try to view the experience in a more favourable light. It would only be for one night after all.

Yet when he thought about it now he realised that there had been something desperate in the way she'd overruled him about the safety thing. She'd hurried him out of the bothy and he'd assumed that it was because she didn't want him around. But now he wondered if there was more to it than that. Perhaps Milla O'Brien wanted time away from the world.

If that was the case then coming to Calcarron would feel like an ordeal, not a pleasure. In some respects it was exactly how he felt himself.

He'd reached the old drover's trail that led across the moors and stopped as a memory seized him. Two carefree boys, racing each other along the track, off to see the standing stones, or to scramble up to the ridge to make dens…

It was a lifetime ago. He could still feel his

friend's presence everywhere, but the images in his mind were smeared with blood now, blurred into memories of dust and death. It wasn't that Duncan was haunting him. He was haunted by the guilt of living—because it should have been him who died, not Duncan.

Even this warm breath of late sun on his face and the sensation of wind in his hair felt too much like living, felt like a betrayal of his friend. What unknowable shift in the cosmos had carved out their fates that day? Why had he been spared? He'd often wondered about that, but his thoughts always tangled into knots.

Losing Duncan had stripped the joy from his life. Sometimes he tried to find solace in the thought that maybe fate had a higher purpose for him, but he didn't feel special enough for such grand designs. If he took the opposite view, and believed that every hand he was dealt, good or bad, was completely random, then it seemed that there wasn't much point to anything, and that scared him even more.

He hadn't expected fate to deal him a wild card like Milla O'Brien. She unsettled him, and fascinated him, but it was a dangerous fascination.

After tomorrow, she wouldn't be his problem any more. He had a busy week ahead and it was going to be hard enough to stay sane without those tantalising green eyes stripping away the veneer he'd so carefully applied since Afghanistan.

He accelerated along the track towards home. He knew his father wanted to talk to him about estate business, or rather, the business of him taking over the estate, but he wasn't ready for that conversation. As the eldest son, his taking over at Calcarron had always been circled on his life map, but he'd never dreamed that that day might come so soon.

He loved this place, and he loved the prospect of being its caretaker sometime in the future, but not yet. He'd built a different life, a life he loved, and leaving it now—especially now—would feel like admitting defeat. It would feel like running away.

He let out the throttle and pushed on faster. Whatever happened, he had to keep his head and stand his ground. If he could make it through the week he'd go back and ask to be reassessed for active duty. The desk job was bleeding him dry. He needed to get back out in the field. He needed to do something that would actually make a difference.

'You mean I'll have to stay at Calcarron House?'

Milla was overwhelmed with disappointment and she hadn't been able to hide it. He'd rescued her at the roadside, so she'd assumed he'd be able to rescue the water situation, but he had been adamant that fixing it would be a long process, although he'd been determinedly vague about the particularities, which had needled her.

'But I don't understand how water can suddenly just stop coming through a pipe...'

He'd shifted on his feet. 'I'm sorry, Milla. I know it's inconvenient, but there's nothing I can do until tomorrow.' He'd thrown her an awkward smile. 'The house isn't all that bad, and at least you won't have to make your own dinner... There's even a studio you can use—' he'd run a hand through his hair '—if you want to work this evening, that is.'

She'd wondered why there was a studio at the house, but she had been too nettled to ask him about it. It had been all she could do to keep her emotions under control.

Cormac had looked genuinely apologetic, and she didn't want to be difficult, but going to stay at the big house was the last thing she wanted to do. She'd have to talk to strangers, and be polite and enthusiastic, and the prospect of such an evening sent her spirits crashing. All the little joys she'd been anticipating about her first night at the bothy were collapsing around her like pillars of salt.

When he'd said he'd go on ahead to make

sure there was a room ready for her she'd been relieved. She needed some time alone to adjust to this new set of circumstances.

As the sound of the quad receded she climbed the stairs to the mezzanine. Cormac had put her holdall at the foot of the bed, and she toyed with the zip. There didn't seem much point in unpacking it now. She sat down on the mattress, then fell backwards and stared at the ceiling.

If only she didn't have to go. This room was a cosy nest and she wanted to hide herself here and never leave. She closed her eyes, then turned over and curled herself into a ball. 'This is all your fault, Dan. Every single bit of it.'

Dan had been in his final year when she'd arrived at St Martin's to start her foundation course. He was a big personality—wild, mercurial—and she'd been surprised that he'd even noticed her. She'd felt unequal to him in every way, but when he'd kissed her that first time, whispered that she was his rock, his port in a storm, she'd felt needed in a way that answered some longing deep within herself.

Her father and her brothers had said he was fake. They'd teased her about his 'Mockney' accent, laughed at the way he knotted his hair into a bun, and they didn't *get* the ink on his arms or the ring through his nose.

Milla had forced herself to ignore them. She

had a small tattoo of a stag inked onto her own
ankle, and a row of piercings made in her left
ear, but deep down she'd hated it that her family wouldn't buy in to her dream of a life with
Daniel Calder-Jones.

She felt sure that her mother would have appreciated Dan's talent, because Colleen O'Brien
had been a teacher and an accomplished artist
in her own right. It was through her mother that
Milla had learned the language and love of art,
discovering a passion which ran through her
own veins too.

After her mother's cancer diagnosis they had
still visited galleries together, Colleen's bald
scalp defiantly wrapped in a brightly coloured
scarf. How she missed her... Milla felt the familiar tears sliding down her face and let them
come.

Dan had relished her family's disapproval—
it had been another layer of drama to fuel his
creativity. He was adept at harnessing the ebb
and flow of his own life and using it to inspire
his art—so good at it, in fact, that he had been
offered a residency in Berlin.

Absorbed with her own postgraduate project,
Milla had encouraged him to go. She'd thought
Berlin, with its vibrant and exciting art scene,
would inspire him, and the international experience and contacts would be good for his career.

The night before he'd left, he'd taken her for dinner at their favourite restaurant and proposed. She'd gazed at him, open-mouthed, while everyone in the restaurant had stilled in anticipation. The thing was, Dan didn't believe in marriage. He'd always said that, and yet there he'd been, gazing at her, waiting for an answer. She'd spluttered a tearful 'yes' and to rapturous applause he'd popped a dazzling diamond ring onto her finger.

She'd been so happy. Finally she'd known where the relationship was going—now her family would have to believe that Daniel Calder-Jones really loved her.

He'd been eager to set a date, so they'd agreed on September—he'd be back by then, and she'd have finished her project. It hadn't left much time to plan a wedding, but she'd thrown herself into it.

She'd found the ideal venue for the country wedding she'd dreamed of—a marquee with pretty bunting. She'd organised a whisky bar for Dan, and trestle tables, wild flowers and traditional music. She had even found the perfect dress—vintage silk and lace with tiny pearls. She'd cried in the bridal boutique because Colleen hadn't been there to tell her how beautiful she looked.

Everything had been falling into place. And

then, three months ago, Dan had flown home unexpectedly to tell her that he'd fallen in love with a German artist called Maria.

Milla had been devastated. To have won his commitment only to lose it again had been too much to bear. She'd stopped eating, stopped sleeping, stopped working.

When her tutor had called her in for a talk she'd ended up crying on his shoulder. He'd advised her to take up photography. He'd suggested taking pictures of anything that caught her eye, for whatever reason. It had been good advice. Instead of trying to create images, she'd spent her days looking for ready-made scenes.

When she'd collated her photographs she had seen a pattern. Pictures of back streets, a single figure in a doorway, a soulful face staring from the window of a café, a couple perched on a broad step, their heads turned in opposite directions...

'You're attracted to loneliness,' her tutor had remarked. 'Your images remind me of Edward Hopper's stuff. You should use them to take your work in a new direction.'

And then he'd handed her a brochure.

'A change of scene might help you get back on track. I've stayed at Strathburn Bothy myself. Peace. Isolation. No phone signal, no internet, no distractions. It might be just what you need.'

She sat up and wiped her cheeks with her hands. She looked around the mezzanine bedroom which she was yet to claim as her own. *Peace. Isolation... No distractions.*

There would be no isolation at Calcarron House, and probably no peace either. As for distractions...

Cormac's eyes stirred in her memory and she pushed the image out of her head. She would try to make the best of it; it was only one night. Tomorrow she'd be back in this room, and her healing process could really begin.

CHAPTER THREE

MILLA CONTEMPLATED THE large stone pillars which flanked the entrance to Calcarron House. She told herself she had no reason to feel nervous; it wasn't her fault that she was imposing on the hospitality of the Buchanan family. It was their bothy, after all, their water pipe malfunction. They should be the ones feeling awkward, not her.

She conjured a memory of her mother smiling. *'Go on with you, now, Milla. You'll be fine.'* Then she threw the four-by-four into gear and drove through the gates onto the long, tree-lined driveway.

On either side giant rhododendron bushes brandished dense clusters of pink and purple flowers, while rabbits scattered in a flash of white tails. After a bend, the driveway emerged from the trees and the house came into view.

Set in substantial grounds of neatly mown grass and flowering shrubs, Calcarron House was an imposing grey stone mansion, its twin turrets reminding Milla of a fairy tale castle in a book she'd owned as a child. Elegant mullioned windows overlooked the gardens towards the loch, and in front, on the wide sweep of immaculate paving, she could see Cormac's silver sports car parked next to a row of four-by-fours.

The house was undeniably grand, and despite her determination not to feel intimidated she felt the butterflies in her stomach start to dance.

With care, she pulled up next to Cormac's car and turned off the engine. She'd barely drawn a breath when she saw him walking towards her. He must have been waiting, looking out for her arrival. The butterflies in her stomach doubled their hectic fluttering.

He opened her door. 'Welcome to Calcarron House.' His smile was hesitant. 'Are you all right with dogs?'

'That depends on the dogs…' In spite of her nerves, she felt a small smile creeping onto her lips. 'If the dogs are all right with me, then I'll be all right with them.'

She saw his mouth twist in amusement, then he motioned to the house. 'In that case, please go on in. My mother's waiting for you. I'll bring your bag.'

In the grand entrance hall she was greeted by three excited Labradors and, behind them, an attractive middle-aged lady with a smile and an outstretched hand.

'Milla, I'm Lily Buchanan. I'm so pleased to meet you and I'm very sorry about the water situation at the bothy. Such a terrible nuisance.'

The light hazel eyes were Cormac's, but in Lily's face they were softened with warmth and gentle empathy. Milla liked her immediately.

'Hello, Mrs Buchanan. It's good to meet you too—and thank you for having me.'

Lily smiled. 'But of course! You're our guest, whether you're staying at the bothy or not… And, please, do call me Lily. Now, come, I'll show you to your room. It's right next to Cormac's grandfather's old studio, so if you're in the habit of working through the night, then carry on. You must do as you please.'

Lily led the way through the flagged hall to a wide oak-panelled staircase, clad in plush blue carpet. The walls above the panelling were hung with traditional landscapes, and some bolder, brighter pieces which caught her eye, but she couldn't stop to look properly because Lily was hastening on, leading her across a sweep of landing and along another corridor.

Finally, she stopped and opened a door. 'Here we are! I hope you like it.'

The room was spacious, and smelled of new fabric and fresh paint. The colour scheme of lilac, heather, moss and peat reminded Milla of a Scottish moorland, and she took delight in the muted tones and welcoming warmth of the textures. The large bed was made up with crisp white bedlinen and a large woollen throw. Mahogany tables gleamed on either side of the bed while a wide matching wardrobe hugged a wall. At the foot of the bed a large leather ottoman glowed in burnished tones, and near the window a wing-backed chair was positioned to take advantage of the view across the hills.

It was a beautiful room and Milla felt a sudden pang of guilt for being so disappointed at the prospect of staying here. She smiled at Lily. 'It's lovely.'

Lily gazed around the room approvingly. 'My daughter Rosie is an interior designer. She's gradually updating all the rooms in the house.'

'Cormac told me she did the bothy too. She's got a good eye.'

'She inherited her artistic talent from her grandfather.' For a moment Lily looked wistful. 'Those are his paintings on the wall.'

Milla stepped closer to look. 'I saw similar paintings in the hall. They're wonderful. I thought they might even be Jolomo's work. I love the bright colours.'

A brief tap on the door signalled Cormac's arrival. Something about the way he moved drew

Milla's eye as he crossed the room and parked her holdall on the ottoman, and she only came back to herself when Lily twitched an imaginary wrinkle out of the curtain.

'Of course you'll be joining us for dinner, won't you, Milla? It will be lovely to have a new face at the table and some fresh conversation. You'll be a nice distraction from all this wedding business—'

'Wedding business?' Lily's words had pulled her up short, but then in a rush she remembered what Mary had said in the shop: *'There's a wedding at the big house on Saturday so we're going to be mobbed.'*

Milla's throat tightened as everything fell into place. Rosie the interior designer was the same Rosie who had been described as making wedding favours with her bridesmaids, the same Rosie who was getting married on Saturday.

Milla tried to swallow. Not only was she staying in a grand house with a family she didn't know but, to add to her discomfort, this was a family in the throes of wedding fever.

She forced herself to smile warmly. 'Oh! How lovely! Who—?'

'Rosie—she's getting married here on Saturday, and to say that it's going to be a big production would be putting it mildly.' Lily exchanged a knowing glance with Cormac. 'Anyway, we'll be serving dinner in fifteen minutes. Cor—could you show Milla the studio before you come down?' She smiled at Milla. 'Then take a few moments to freshen up, if you like. The en suite bathroom is through that door over there.'

Cormac wasn't sure if it was a trick of the light, or a trick of his imagination, but Milla's face seemed paler than before, her eyes a deeper green, like the green of shady water. She looked preoccupied. She seemed barely interested in the tour of his grandfather's studio and yet again he felt at a loss for what to say.

He tugged open a shallow drawer in a wide unit and lifted out a sheaf of paper. 'There's heavyweight paper in here...spare sketch-books...' He rummaged around a bit. 'All kinds of stuff in these drawers—you'll know better than me what it's for...'

'Thanks...' She glanced at the paper. 'I'll take a look if I decide to...to sketch something, but probably I won't be drawing anything.' She shrugged. 'I mean, there won't be much time for drawing because I'll be going back to the bothy first thing in the morning, when you've sorted out the water.'

He pushed the drawer shut and turned away. He didn't know what had darkened her mood, but he sensed a deep discontent within her which was going to make his next job more difficult. He'd felt sure that the news he had to relay would have been better coming from his mother, but Lily had reasoned that since Milla was already acquainted with him, *he* should be the one to tell her about the marquee.

He forced a neutral expression onto his face and turned around. 'Look, Milla, I'm sorry but I'm afraid there's going to be a bit of a delay with the water.'

He saw a flash of desperation colour her eyes, then watched as her gaze hardened. 'What do you mean, "a bit of a delay"? Why?'

'The marquee company called. Apparently they've been asked to supply five huge tents for a rock festival in Inverness. They can only do that if they bring Rosie's marquee a day early, so it's coming tomorrow morning and I'll have to stay here until it's rigged.'

She took a step towards him. 'But…but if the marquee company are doing the rigging, why do you have to be here?'

He tried to soften his expression. 'Because it's what I came back for—to oversee the exterior operations. The marquee, the generators, the lighting. I've got to make sure everything dovetails, that all Rosie's designs come to life. She's counting on me.'

'And where does that leave me? Who do I count on?'

The vehemence in her voice surprised him, but it didn't change anything. 'In normal circumstances I'd be prioritising the water at the bothy, but it's just bad luck, Milla. I'm really sorry, but there's nothing we can do except offer you the very best hospitality we can whilst you're here, including the use of this studio and any materials that you need. It's only a day.' He looked around at the room his grandfather had loved. 'I don't see what's so terrible about being here.'

She tilted her chin, fixing lustrous eyes on his. 'I never said it was terrible; it's just not what I was expecting. I thought I was going to be at Strathburn on my own, working, and instead I'm here, caught on the fringes of—'

He saw that chink of vulnerability in her eyes and he couldn't help his curiosity. 'On the fringes of what…?'

Her fingers drifted to the hem of her tee shirt, then she thrust them into the pockets of her jeans. 'Of a wedding, was what I was going to say…' Her gaze fell to the floor. 'I'm just not big on the whole wedding thing, okay?'

'I'll try not to propose, then…'

She jerked up her head and frowned. 'Was that meant to be funny?'

He shrugged. He wasn't quite sure what had made him say it. It certainly sounded like the kind of dry humour he'd used to be famous for. There had been a time when he could crack up his whole team with a well-timed one-liner, and he'd made Duncan laugh all the time. Maybe he had been trying to make her smile, because her smile was so much better than her frown.

She sighed and turned her attention to the wide unit, pulling open the drawers in turn. 'All that fuss and bother…endless planning and dreaming…and after all that it might rain on your wedding day, or maybe the groom might not even show up. I mean, what's it all about?'

It seemed to Cormac that she might be talking about herself. Involuntarily, his eyes darted to her left hand. 'I'm assuming that's a rhetorical question?'

Perhaps she hadn't heard him, or perhaps she chose not to answer. He watched her as she poked around in the lower drawer. A cluster of fine blonde strands nestled in the soft nape of her neck and he moistened his lips. Perhaps she'd been let down or stood up at the altar, or something like that. It was probable that the jerk who'd messed her about wasn't even worthy to kiss the ground she walked on, but Milla's history was none of his business.

As if she could feel his eyes on her, she closed the drawer and stood up. 'I'm sorry for moaning. I really hope that your sister has a lovely wedding. But the thought of trying to work in a house with all that going on—honestly, it fills me with dread.'

'Dread? That's a strong emotion...' He wished he could see inside her head, see what she was thinking. It was hard to know what to say.

His eyes travelled around the room and came to rest on his grandfather's easel.

He tried to sound conciliatory. 'If you're anything like my grandfather, once you're working you won't even know what day of the week is...'

Something in her expression chased his smile away. He couldn't make her out, and suddenly he wondered why he was even trying.

He glanced at his watch. 'We should go down.' He walked to the door and held it open for her. 'I'm sure you'll feel better about staying here once you've met everyone.'

'Perhaps.' She walked past him, then stopped at the bedroom door. 'I'm sorry—that sounded so rude.' She lifted her eyes to his. 'I'm grateful, of course, it's just...'

'Just that you're not big on the whole wedding thing—I get it.'

She nodded. 'I… I need a moment to freshen up, if that's okay, and then I'll be down.'

'Of course. Take as long as you need.'

As she closed the door behind her he blew out a long breath. He'd known breaking the news about the water would be difficult, but he hadn't bargained for this aversion she seemed to have for weddings.

He knew that such a reaction could only have its roots in some deep hurt. Hadn't he been filled with hate for the snipers who'd killed Duncan? A hate that had burned in his heart for so long that sometimes he could taste its ash in his mouth. He pictured Milla's eyes, that fleeting vulnerability, the small tremble in her chin, and he wondered who could have wounded her so badly.

He shook himself and started along the corridor towards the stairs. He couldn't indulge his curiosity about Milla O'Brien. Being curious about anyone was dangerous. It opened doors to other feelings, might lead to entanglements and confusion, and he had enough confusion in his head already.

If she was averse to 'the whole wedding thing', then he'd try his best to steer the dinner conversation into safer territory. People generally enjoyed talking about their passions, so he'd

ask her about her work and her inspirations…
It was the only thing he could do.

Milla sank onto the ottoman and stared at the
view of darkening hills through the window.
She couldn't believe how her plans had been
upended. The water problem had been a major
blow, but now she would have to endure dinner
with Cormac's family, where the main topic of
conversation was bound to be Rosie's 'big production' of a wedding.

In the studio, when she'd tried to tell Cormac how she felt, he'd just made a lame joke
about not proposing to her. When she'd tried
again he'd simply shrugged it off, told her she
wouldn't notice anything once she was working.

Practically everything that came out of Cormac's mouth felt like a polite brush-off. He was
cool and measured in a way that she struggled
to be.

She unzipped her holdall and pulled out a
silky blouse. It was the only smart thing she'd
brought, so it would have to do. In front of
the bathroom mirror, she tidied her hair and
splashed her face.

Dinner was going to be an ordeal. She would
have to smile and show interest in Rosie's perfect wedding, even though she was crumpling
inside.

She drew in a deep breath and pinched her cheeks to draw up the colour. Her mother had used the same trick when she'd been pale and sick from the chemo but had wanted people to think she was fine; it had been a selfless masquerade to spare others the pain of observing her decline. Milla couldn't pretend to have such a noble motivation, but if her mother had managed it, then so could she.

'So, Milla, what kind of work do you do?'

She didn't want to talk about her work, but the timing was perfect. Cormac's question had cut across the conversation, interrupting Rosie, who had been trying to engage her in a discussion about trends in wedding décor.

She put down her soup spoon and blotted her mouth with her napkin. She didn't know what to say; she couldn't very well tell him that she'd lost her way, artistically, and was trying to make something of urban portraiture when her natural inclination was towards landscape.

She felt the colour creeping into her cheeks as all eyes at the table turned in her direction.

She smiled. 'I'm basically a fine art person, but at the moment I'm experimenting with a few different things…'

Her pulse climbed as Cormac looked at her. 'Different things? Like what?'

She broke away from his gaze and looked across the table at Sam. Cormac's younger brother was twenty, gangly in the way that young men often were before they settled into their shape. His hair was lighter and redder than Cormac's, his eyes blue and mischievous.

'Mostly portraiture...'

Sam smiled sweetly. 'I could model for you, if you like... I have very good cheekbones.'

'Set in a very big head,' Rosie added.

Milla laughed. 'Thank you for the offer, Sam, but I'm working from photographs I took in London.'

'Ah...so you're painting yuppies, or guppies, or whatever they call themselves these days...'

Cormac's father, Alasdair, had the same twinkle in his eye that she'd seen in Cormac's once or twice.

She shook her head. 'No. They're not yuppie types...just faces, really...random faces I'm using.'

'But you must have a thread...something which connects them...?'

Cormac's voice pulled her back. He seemed relentless in his pursuit, his questions pinning her down, forcing her to find answers she didn't have.

She remembered her tutor's words about what he thought he'd seen in her photographs. 'I suppose the theme would have something to do with loneliness…my faces are all sad faces.'

Did she see his eyes cloud for an instant? Whatever she saw there made her head spin, so that she had to look away again, but even as she caught Sam's eye she could feel the latent heat of Cormac's gaze on her skin.

Sam tore a piece from his bread roll and buttered it with gusto. 'Why do artists never paint happy people? In every painting I can think of the faces run the whole gamut of emotions from slightly miffed to utterly miserable—no one smiles.'

'Except for the Mona Lisa,' said Lily.

Sam put down his knife. 'That's not a smile—it's a grimace…'

Milla picked up her spoon. She was glad that the conversation was shifting focus. She needed to eat something, even if Cormac's presence across the table was unsettling. If she glanced up he invariably glanced up too, so that their eyes locked, and then she would feel giddy and have to look away. She couldn't tally the heat in his eyes with the coolness of his tone, or fathom his long silences along with his casual interjections whenever the conversation turned to wedding matters.

When Rosie started talking about the different-flavoured tiers she'd chosen for her wedding cake Milla found her thoughts drifting to the surprise cake she'd been planning for Dan. She'd seen the idea in a magazine and known he'd love it. A 'Man Cake', it had been called—a pork pie base layer, topped with a round of Stilton and decorated with fresh figs and grapes. It had been such a simple idea, but she'd been so excited about it and hadn't been able to wait to see his face on the day.

Now she never would.

She looked down at her uneaten cheesecake just as Cormac suddenly put down his fork and spoon.

'For goodness' sake, Rosie, will you leave us some surprises? The way you're going, we'll have lived this day ten times over before it's even arrived.'

As a hush descended over the table, Milla was gripped by a realisation and slowly lifted her eyes to his face. He'd been doing it for her— the interruptions and distractions. All through dinner, every time someone had started talking about the wedding, he'd tried to change the subject. He'd asked her a question about her work, or asked his father something about the estate.

She felt a rush of conflicting emotion. All this time she'd thought he was being heavy-handed, but he'd spent the entire evening trying to protect her from Rosie's wedding.

He glanced at her, then turned back to his family and ran a hand through his hair. 'I'm sorry, Rosie, I didn't mean it to come out like that. It's just—'

Milla watched Rosie blinking in faint bewilderment, and then, to her surprise, she saw the girl's lips curve upwards into a smile.

'Oh, my God, it's actually happened…'

Sam looked at his sister with curious eyes. 'What's happened?'

Rosie shook her head and laughed. 'I've turned into a Bridezilla.'

CHAPTER FOUR

THE CHURCH DOORS peeled back and she squeezed her father's arm. He threw her a nervous smile.

'Here we go, love. Hold on tight.'

She looked down at the bouquet in her hand, then lifted her eyes to take in the scene as they began their slow walk up the aisle. Faces turned towards them...she enjoyed their admiration, their happy smiles.

She looked ahead, tried to catch a glimpse of him. But the aisle was long and she couldn't quite see.

A gentle rain started to fall, and she giggled as tiny water drops clung to her eyelashes and peppered the roses in her bouquet.

Then the rain fell harder, causing the posies on the pew ends to droop on their ribbons.

She looked down, saw that she was stepping through mud. It was ruining her bridal shoes, splattering the front of her dress.

Her father and the guests had disappeared,

*and she was trying to lift her dress clear of the
mud. But it was too heavy and she could barely
move.*

*She dropped her bouquet and she was cry-
ing, tugging at her dress, trying to walk. But
she was stuck. She looked for the groom, but
the minister was alone.*

*He walked towards her, shaking his head.
'Why are you here...?'*

Milla gasped and opened her eyes. Her heart
was pounding in her throat and it took a few moments for her to realise that she'd been dreaming. The church, the rain, the mud, the absent
bridegroom—none of it was real. She shuddered
with relief and wiped her wet cheeks with her
palms. At least Dan had broken up with her before things had gone that far. Perhaps, in a way,
she'd been lucky.

The nightmare faded as she listened to the
sounds of the unfamiliar house. Footsteps on
the flagstones in the hall, a bump, a dog whining, and outside the vibration of a lawnmower.

Her thoughts turned to the events of the previous evening. After everyone had stopped
laughing at Rosie's 'Bridezilla' revelation,
she'd felt confused and awkward. She hadn't
wanted to meet Cormac's eye again, and she'd
had the feeling that he hadn't wanted to look
at her either.

Over coffee, she'd focused her attention on Sam, and when she'd glanced across the table again Cormac's seat had been empty.

She thought about the bothy, how different she'd be feeling now if she'd woken up in that mezzanine room, with nothing but quiet for company. In this house she was a stranger, and facing the family at breakfast—especially Cormac—was the last thing she wanted to do.

The family always breakfasted in the kitchen, Lily had told her the previous night, and it was *ad hoc*, so she was to come down in her own time and help herself to whatever she wanted to eat.

Whilst Milla appreciated the informality, the thought of poking around in the kitchen, looking for coffee and cereal, was a little daunting, so she was relieved to find Lily sitting at the table with a newspaper when she pushed open the door.

'Good morning, dear.' Lily looked serene in a blue cashmere sweater. 'Did you sleep well?'

'Yes, thank you.' Milla pushed the upsetting dream out of her head and smiled. 'I was very comfortable.'

'I'm glad. Can I get you some tea or coffee?'

'Coffee would be great, thanks.'

Lily rose and poured a mug of coffee from

a cafetière parked on the warming plate of the
range. She set it down on the table and smiled.
'I can't believe how much work is involved in
hosting a wedding. Every time I think it's under
control, I remember something else—in fact,
I need to go and call the florist right now, so
you'll have to fend for yourself.'

She motioned to the stove.

'There's porridge, if you like, or cereal in the
larder, or you can make toast if you want. Just
dive in.'

She smiled, then disappeared through the
door.

Milla tipped milk into her coffee, then sat
down at the scrubbed pine table and wrapped
her hands around the steaming mug. She could
hear movement elsewhere in the house, but
there was no sign of Cormac and she felt relieved. Last night it had seemed to her that he
was going out of his way to shield her from
Rosie's wedding talk, but now she wondered if
she'd been imagining it. Maybe it had been exactly as he'd said. He was simply tired of hearing about every detail and would rather enjoy
the wedding day when it arrived.

In the cold light of day, she was forced to
admit that that made more sense.

She sipped her coffee and looked around. A
tall dresser was crammed with china while an

assortment of well-used pots and pans dangled from a rack over the cooker. Nothing in the room matched, but everything fitted perfectly, and in spite of its large size it felt cosy and inviting—unlike Dan's parents' kitchen.

Dan's family home in London might have slipped from the pages of an upmarket magazine: glass tables, pale carpets and carefully placed *objets d'art*. The kitchen had been white and minimalist, the sleek lines of its pristine counters interrupted only by an occasional mystifying gadget. By contrast, this kitchen felt inhabited. The wooden chopping boards stacked against the tiles were knife-scored, the calendar on the wall was inked and circled, and the storage tins on the counter were faded with use. This kitchen spoke of life and love.

There was something about it that reminded Milla of her mother and she felt a fresh wave of loss breaking over her heart.

When she heard approaching footsteps she thought Lily must be returning, but it was Cormac who came through the door—Cormac, whose presence caused her breath to catch and the colour to creep into her cheeks.

He'd obviously been out running. His grey tee shirt was patchy with sweat and his arms and legs were sheened with perspiration.

At the sight of her he stopped. 'Oh, hello…' He smiled slightly, his eyes wary. 'I mean, good morning. Did you sleep well?'

'Yes, I did…' She caught herself noticing the smooth curve of his bicep and forced herself to meet his gaze. 'Thank you for asking.'

At the sink, he filled a glass with water and drank it down, then swiped the moisture from his brow with the back of his hand. 'Good.' His eyes lingered on hers for a moment, then he turned away to refill his glass.

The hair at the back of his neck looked damp. She wondered if he could sense her eyes travelling over the curve of his shoulder blades and down his back to his narrow hips and muscular legs. When he turned around again she pretended she'd been occupied with the newspaper.

He sipped his water. 'It was raining when I set out this morning…but it's stopped now.' He glanced at the newspaper. 'It might even turn out fine, which'll make things easier for putting up the marquee.'

Milla felt hope tingling in her veins. 'You mean it might go quickly? That you might have time to—?'

'Please, Milla—' He frowned, and suddenly she felt she was being a nuisance. 'What I said about the weather and the marquee… I wasn't implying that I'd be able to…' He sipped from his glass again and shrugged. 'I was just trying to make conversation.'

She sighed under her breath. She hadn't been trying to push him about fixing the water, but when he'd mentioned the marquee it had tipped her into her dark place, triggered a memory about her own marquee. That excruciating phone call she'd had to make cancelling the booking, and the ensuing discussion about how much of her deposit she could expect to get back.

She rose from the table and carried her empty mug to the sink. He stepped aside, the fresh scent of his skin lingering in the air and throwing her a little off-balance.

To avoid meeting his gaze she busied herself rinsing out her mug. 'I wasn't trying to pressurise you—it's just that I've got to get my work finished for an exhibition and I'm already behind. I came to Scotland to get on with it, and this whole water thing has thrown a spanner in the works.'

She threw him a glance, detected a momentary softening of his expression.

'I understand, but it's only one day. It'll pass, and before you know it you'll be back at the bothy.' He put his glass down. 'I'm going to shower. If you need anything, just let us know.'

* * *

In the studio, Milla busied herself pulling materials out of the drawers she'd perused the day before. But even after she'd arranged paints and palettes on a bench, and pulled the easel into the best light near the window, she couldn't shake off the restless disappointment she was feeling about the bothy.

This studio was a good space, and the Buchanan family had been nothing but hospitable, but she still felt intimidated by the grandness of Calcarron House and disconcerted by her feelings about Cormac.

In the kitchen she'd felt an awareness of him which had bordered on attraction and she couldn't make sense of it. How could she be feeling such a thing when she was still bruised from her broken engagement and when Cormac himself was so unfathomable? The stilted way he spoke to her and the deliberate air of indifference he adopted whenever they were alone conflicted with what she thought she could see in his eyes, and the whole business was messing with her head.

She stared at the materials she'd laid out on the bench. If she could just lose herself in work, then she'd be able to push Cormac out of her thoughts. She pulled her cardigan tighter and reached for a sketchbook. Her folio of photographs was up at the bothy. Could she work from memory?

She'd just put pencil to paper when there was a knock on the door. When she opened it she found Sam in the hallway, clutching a huge basket of logs.

'Hi, Milla! Cor asked me to bring you some logs for the fire. He said it was cold in here.'

Bemused, she stepped back to let him pass. 'That's very thoughtful of him—and kind of you to bring them. Thank you.'

He hefted the basket over to the hearth and set it down. 'Grandad always kept a fire burning in here—it doesn't get any sun, you see, and… Well, the room's been empty for a while.' He looked momentarily wistful, then brightened. 'Would you like me to light a fire for you now?'

'That would be great—but only if you've got time. I know you're busy today.'

Sam grinned. 'It's fine. Cor's dealing with the marquee team. He's in his element, ordering them about. It's his thing, after all.'

Milla was curious. Cormac was an enigma to her—perhaps if she knew more about him it would help her deal with him.

She tried to sound casual. 'His "thing"? What's that, then? He told me he runs errands.'

Sam laughed roundly. 'Cor's got a dry sense

of humour—I can just imagine him saying that!' He struck a match and set it to the kindling in the hearth. 'He's a Troop Commander in the Royal Engineers.'

Suddenly everything fell into place—the purposeful stride, the tanned arms and close-cropped hair. His instruction about the tyre— *'Be sure to have that fixed.'* The conversation she'd overheard in the shop—*'I see Cormac's back for the wedding, then.'*

She felt a smile warming her lips. Cormac was, indeed, wryly humorous, and for some reason this insight into his character satisfied her.

'So, where's he based?'

'He's on leave at the moment, from Chatham Barracks, but before that he was in Afghanistan.' A glimmer of discomfort coloured Sam's eyes, as if he'd said too much.

She smiled. 'Well, after Afghanistan I'm sure putting up a wedding marquee will be a walk in the park.'

Sam rose to his feet and grinned. 'You're joking, right? Rosie Buchanan is more exacting than the Commander-in-Chief himself.'

'Well, I suppose getting married is a big thing.' Milla tried to meet Sam's gaze squarely. 'She wants everything to be perfect—I can understand that.'

* * *

When Sam had gone, Milla returned to her sketchbook, but her thoughts quickly wandered. Cormac had sent Sam with firewood so that she wouldn't be cold—he must have come in earlier to check the temperature in the room. She supposed checking such things was par for the course in a house used for hospitality; it didn't mean he'd been thinking about her in any special way.

She picked up her pencil, gazed at it blankly, then threw it down. The room *was* cool—no wonder she couldn't concentrate. She'd have to wait for it to warm up.

To fill time, she crossed to the bookcase and inspected a collection of photos in silver frames. They were mostly family pictures, and photos of shooting parties, but there was one in particular that caught her eye and she lifted it into the light to look more closely.

Taken in the desert, it was a photograph of Cormac and a friend in fatigues—arms slung around each other's shoulders, all sunshine and wide smiles. She gazed at Cormac's face, marvelling that he could own such a smile. Certainly she'd never seen it.

She put the frame back and rubbed at her arms. She hadn't been surprised to discover that he was in the military. He had the honed physique and powerful air of the ultra-fit. Sam had sounded awkward about Afghanistan, though, and it sparked a memory of what she'd over-heard in the village shop—something about Cormac *'not being right'.*

Mary had said something else too… *'He'll have to let it go sooner or later…you can't carry that stuff around with you for ever.'*

Milla's heart stalled. Something bad must have happened—something that burdened him with the weight of sadness she'd seen in his eyes when he'd stopped to help her on the road.

She felt a strange shifting sensation beneath her feet. Standing in front of the fire he'd ar-ranged for her, all of her preconceptions about Cormac started to shuffle like a deck of cards. She'd been gazing through the lens of her own sadness for so long that it had made her blind. Cormac was adept at maintaining a polite dis-tance, but for the first time since she'd met him she began to realise that, just like her, he might have reasons for being the way he appeared to be.

'Milla's cute.'

The memory of Milla pretending to read the upside-down newspaper on the kitchen table made Cormac want to laugh, but the impulse drained away when he remembered how unsure of himself he felt in her company, how guarded he had to be. Even the simplest conversation felt like a minefield; he never knew where it was safe to tread.

He slotted the leg beam into the base plate of the marquee and tried to sound ambivalent. 'She's temperamental, is what you mean.'

Sam shook his head. 'Not at all. She's lovely.'

Cormac looked up, saw his brother's eyes gleaming with a familiar devilment.

'Maybe she just prefers me to you.'

He remembered Milla chatting to Sam at the dinner table the night before, their effortless amiability. 'That's highly likely.'

'She seemed quite touched that you'd sent me up with logs for the fire, though.' Sam's gaze was loaded. 'She said to thank you.'

He knew what Sam was driving at and he felt his patience wearing thin. 'The room needed an airing, that's all. Look, I think the guys need some help over there.'

Sam sighed. 'Righto. I'll see you in a bit.'

Cormac watched Sam's back as he walked away. His brother was only trying to nudge him into the light. It was what they all tried to do, every time he was here. They wanted him to draw a line under what had happened and move on, but he couldn't turn off his grief with a switch.

That was why he didn't come back to Cal-carron very often. He knew his family was concerned about him, but he couldn't bear the weight of their subtle scrutiny, turning him over, looking for signs that he was on the mend. He wouldn't mend, and he wished they'd accept it the way he'd accepted it.

Seeing his best friend cut down right in front of him was an image he couldn't shake off, but he'd had to hold it together that day for the sake of his men. He'd stowed his anguish and fol-lowed procedure, got them to safety, brought Duncan's body home.

He'd devised a strategy for coping. The trick was to keep the world at arm's length, to stay locked down tight and not let anyone in.

That was why Milla unsettled him. What-ever hurt she'd suffered that made her so touchy about weddings had stirred his protective in-stincts. The pain she'd tried to hide had diverted his attention from his own burdens and moved him to help her. After his outburst at dinner, the look in her eye had told him that she knew what he'd been doing. For the first time since Dun-can's death he'd been blown wide open, and he'd had to escape. He hadn't been able to bear to meet her eye again for fear that next time she'd see right through him.

He picked up another cross-brace, grateful

for the physical work. Concentrating on one task after another would stop him thinking. Thinking only tied him in knots. Afghanistan, pressure from his father about taking over at Calcarron and now, quite unexpectedly, Milla O'Brien. Better to focus on constructing the marquee. Much safer.

Milla's pencil rasped across the sketchpad, the lines and arcs forming a cheekbone, an eye socket, a nose. A sudden dog's bark startled her, and her pencil threw out a jagged line. She sighed, blew a strand of hair off her face and worked an eraser over the paper.

Since Sam had brought the firewood no one had disturbed her, but she could feel a restless energy thrumming through the walls of the great house, and the random yells, clangs and barking from outside were distracting. If she'd been at the bothy...

But why even think about that? She was a guest at Calcarron House and, as such, she felt like a fish out of water.

She threw down her sketchpad and walked to the window. Cormac had been right—the day was turning out to be fine. Perhaps a walk would help, and when she got back she'd make a cup of tea and bring it up. Two small acts of independence, but absolutely necessary if she was going to survive until tomorrow.

Grabbing a jacket from her room, she crept along the corridor and padded quietly down the grand staircase. From a room off the main hall she could hear Lily on the telephone, and from a room close by the sound of confident female voices—Rosie and her bridesmaids. When she heard footsteps on the move she hurried through the main door. She didn't want to bump into anyone.

Outside, a faint warmth teased the sweet fragrance of damp grass into the air. If the clouds lifted it would be a lovely day. Self-consciously, she picked her way along a path leading from the house across the wide lawn. Some distance away, the marquee team were assembling the vast metal frame, but she kept her eyes forward, trying not to think about the traditional canvas marquee she'd chosen for her own wedding.

The dogs ran across the lawn to greet her, then trailed along beside her as she left the garden and joined a track leading into the stretch of woodland that ran alongside the loch. As she walked through green shade, breathing in the soft air, she felt the tension sliding from her shoulders.

She watched the dogs snuffling through tall ferns and bramble thickets, felt the first rays of sunshine filtering through the clouds and for the first time since she'd arrived felt happy. She walked on, enjoying the rhythm of her own stride and the sound of birds in the trees.

When the path merged with the loch shore at a small, stony beach the dogs ran into the water and stumbled about in the shallows with wagging tails and dripping tongues.

Milla made her way over the stones to a large boulder, where she could sit and take in the view. From here, looking back, she could see how grand Calcarron House really was. The prospect of owning it one day should make Cormac happy, yet he seemed not to be, and she wondered why.

A sudden shaft of sunlight split the clouds over the loch and she shook Cormac out of her head. She had enough problems of her own—not least of which was recording this spectacular fusion of light and landscape before the breeze lifted the cloud away. She patted her pockets and felt a glow of satisfaction. It was a useful habit she'd cultivated, to keep a small sketchbook and pencil in every jacket she owned.

She flipped to a new page and started to sketch the house, the loch and the mountains in all that glorious light.

By the time she'd finished the dogs were dozing in the shade. She hadn't been inclined to rush back because she'd been enjoying the sound of the water and the sight of the shifting skies, but now she was stiff from sitting and hungry too. She pocketed her sketchbook and eased herself off the rock, planting her feet on a stable boulder beneath.

Alerted by her movement, the dogs scrambled up and bounded across to see her, tails wagging with excitement.

'Steady on, you silly creatures, you're going to—'

But it was too late. Their clamouring bodies were knocking her off balance. Her left foot slipped into the water and then she was falling sideways, barely having time to cry out in pain before she landed on the stones.

The marquee was up and the jubilant crew had downed tools to go for a tea break. Cormac was about to follow them inside when he caught sight of the dogs, trotting across the lawn towards him. He frowned and looked past them to the edge of the grounds, where the path disappeared into the woods. He'd seen Milla heading that way a couple of hours ago, with the dogs in tow, but there was no sign of her following them back.

When Tyler arrived at his side he rubbed the broad black head, but the dog pulled away and nosed his hand, whining softly. Cormac dropped to his knees and fondled the dog's ears.

'What is it, boy? Where's Milla? Did you leave her behind?'

Tyler pawed his arm and whined again.

Once more Cormac looked across the lawn towards the trees, searching for Milla's bright red jacket, but there was no sign of her. He rose to his feet and sighed. She was probably just dawdling, but the dog was acting strangely— strangely enough for his sense of duty to kick in. He'd go and check to see if she was coming. If he saw her, he could always retreat, then she'd never know he'd been looking for her.

With the dogs at his heels he struck out across the lawn. He moved quickly along the track, scanning from left to right, but there was no sign of her. He tried to calculate how far she could have walked in a couple of hours, and was resigning himself to a long search when suddenly he caught a flash of red on the path up ahead.

He stopped, shrank back, then slipped off the path into the cover of the trees. He felt ridiculous, creeping about like this, but he didn't want her to misconstrue his intentions. The dogs had come back without her, which was obviously a cause for concern. He told himself that anyone would be doing what he was doing—checking to make sure that a guest was all right. He was concerned for her wellbeing, nothing more.

He moved through the trees until he could see her more clearly. At first he thought she was sitting on a fallen log for a rest, but as he drew nearer he saw that her head and left hand were bloodied.

'Milla!'

Without thinking, he broke cover and ran through the trees towards her. At the sound of his voice, she looked up with visible relief.

He reached her side, his heart pounding. 'Are you okay? What happened?'

'I slipped on the rocks near the edge of the loch.' She smiled weakly. 'I'm mighty glad to see you.'

He reached his fingers to her head. 'May I?'

She moistened her lips and nodded. With a gentle finger he lifted the hair away from her forehead. There was a bruise, but the skin wasn't broken. The smears of blood must have come from her hand. He opened her palm and examined the cut.

'It probably stings, but it's nothing much.'

She winced. 'I know—"'tis but a scratch."'

Before he could stop himself he was smiling. '"'Tis but a flesh wound."'

She laughed softly. 'You like Monty Python too.'

There was a gentle light in her eyes as she

looked at him, a warmth in her voice that he hadn't noticed before. He felt an explicable desire to touch her face, tuck the stray lock of hair behind her ear—the ear with those tiny studs which seemed to him like an insult to perfection.

He caught himself drifting and quickly rose to his feet. 'Come on. We should go and clean up that cut.'

She shook her head slowly. 'I can't walk very well.'

'What do you mean?'

'When I fell I wrenched my ankle. That's the real problem. I've been hobbling down this path for ages, but I had to stop and rest because it hurt.'

Finally everything made sense. No wonder she'd looked so relieved when he'd arrived.

He drew in a breath. 'Put your arms around my neck.'

'You're going to carry me?'

'Well, I'm not calling the air ambulance. I can carry you, but you need to hold on.'

'Okay.'

Her tone was reluctant, but he felt her arms sliding around his neck and he swung her up. She wasn't heavy and settled naturally against him, as if she belonged there.

He adjusted his hold slightly. 'How's that?'

Her voice was husky. 'It's okay.'

Their faces were inches apart and for a moment he felt his senses swim. He forced himself to look ahead and start walking. He felt her grip tighten around his shoulders, noticed that her delicate fingers were curled into fists. Bemused, he focused on the dogs and the ruts in the track.

'It's a good thing that you were passing by...'

Her tone was casual, but he could read her intent. She was letting him know that she knew he'd come looking for her. He wondered how she always managed to lay him bare.

'The dogs came back without you.'

'I didn't think anyone had noticed me leaving.'

He squinted at her. 'You walked across the lawn in a bright red jacket.'

'Ah! Of course.'

He walked on through the trees, his powerful strides taking them upwards as the path diverted around a rocky outcrop. He felt her eyes on his face.

'You're strong. Do you work at it?'

He stepped over an exposed tree root. He couldn't very well dodge her question when she was fused closer to him than his own shadow. 'I have to be fit...for my job.'

'Oh, right—Sam mentioned it. You're in the Army—a captain or something.'

'Troop Commander—I'm in the Engineers.'
He wondered what else Sam had told her.

'Well, it's lucky for me that you're so— Can
I rest my head against you? It's kind of hard,
holding it away.'

She didn't wait for him to answer but dropped
her head against his. Her hair felt soft on his
cheek, the clean scent of it filling his nostrils
while her breath warmed his neck. He didn't
want to like it so much and lifted his head a little
higher, ordering himself to ignore the sensory
overload that was Milla O'Brien.

He felt her cheeks lifting into a smile. 'I might
have guessed you were a commander.'

'Why?'

'When you ordered me to get my wheel fixed
you were kind of bossy.'

He tried to stop the smile twitching at the
edges of his lips. 'It's important to have a working spare.'

'I know that. My father's a motor mechanic.'

He laughed. 'No surprise there.'

'How so?'

'Not many girls I know can talk so knowl-
edgeably about air ratchets.'

As she dropped her head against his and gave
herself up to the rhythm of his stride Milla gritted her teeth against the pain in her ankle. Such

a silly accident, getting tangled up with the dogs and losing her footing.

After the fall, when she'd tried to get up and realised what she'd done, she'd felt crushed—and not only because of the pain. She knew that Cormac's family would never let her move to the bothy if she couldn't walk, and the thought of staying at Calcarron House for even longer filled her with dismay.

If only she'd stayed in the studio instead of venturing out she wouldn't be in this hopeless situation.

The movement of Cormac's body against hers was playing havoc with her senses. The smell of his skin...the warm shift of his muscles as he held her. She had a curious urge to touch him, so she clenched her hands into fists so that she couldn't—not even by accident. But there was something else bothering her as well.

When she'd heard his call, seen him running towards her, she'd felt strangely elated that he'd come to find her. The look she'd seen on his face... There'd been something intense about that moment, and when he'd lifted her into his arms she'd felt a deep contentment. Had Dan ever made her feel like that? She couldn't seem to remember.

To interrupt her chaotic thoughts, she said, 'Thanks for sending up the firewood.'

He glanced at her, then looked ahead. 'It was nothing. The studio was cold—it's not been used since my grandfather passed...'

His voice trailed away and Milla reflected on the hollow months after her mother's death. The half-finished painting on the easel that they couldn't bear to move; the floral wellingtons in the hall, gradually filling with spiders' webs.

She pushed the memories away. 'Lily was showing me some of your grandfather's work. He was talented.'

Cormac's voice faltered. 'He never thought so, but he loved painting.'

They were coming out of the trees now, and the dogs scampered ahead towards the terrace where Cormac's family appeared to be having afternoon tea. Seized by a sudden fear, Milla jerked her head away from his shoulder.

'Cor, I really don't want a lot of fuss made about my fall—I already feel like an idiot. Do we have to go this way, right in front of everyone?'

She'd called him *Cor*. It had tripped off her tongue so naturally that she hadn't had time to stop herself. Had he noticed? Being held in his arms must have tricked her brain—it felt so comfortable after all—but she hadn't meant to sound so familiar.

He stopped walking and they both looked

across the lawn to where Lily was standing, her hand raised in a wave.

He shot her a glance. 'Yes, we do, I'm afraid, because it looks like we've been spotted.'

'There must be so much to do on a big estate like this, Alasdair—do you have any help?'

Cormac admired the way Milla was managing the conversation at dinner. Her endless questions about Calcarron were deflecting attention away from herself *and* away from Rosie's wedding.

His father put down his knife and fork. 'We do, Milla. We have a gamekeeper, and he has a couple of lads helping at busy times, but the *family* is very hands-on at Calcarron.'

He directed a pointed gaze at Cormac and Cormac looked down at his wine glass. He wished his father would let the subject go. He couldn't so easily slip into rural life after Afghanistan. He was an engineer, not a fighter, but he had a score to settle for Duncan. He didn't know exactly how he was going to settle it, but while this rage and grief was boiling inside him he couldn't come back here.

'Estate management is demanding in many ways. We've got a lot on right now, maintaining the moorland for grouse—we rely on income from shooting parties, you see.'

'I thought moorland grew wild,' Milla said. 'How do you maintain it?'

'We burn the heather from time to time—don't we, Cor?'

Cormac swallowed a mouthful of red wine and put his glass down. 'Yes.' He looked at his father, then at Milla. 'Grouse feed on new heather shoots, so we burn back the old so that new plants can grow.'

'Those shooting parties must love staying here.'

At first Milla's remark struck Cormac as ironic, given that she wanted to leave as soon as possible, and then he remembered that her reasons for wanting to go had nothing to do with the house itself.

He smiled. 'Yes, they do. Staying at Calcarron is a big draw. The location is... Well, you've seen for yourself.'

As the conversation continued Cormac relaxed into his chair and watched Milla out of the corner of his eye. When he'd lifted her into his arms he'd only been thinking of getting her back to the house safely, but he could still feel her hair against his cheek, her body against his, and it felt like a sweet torment.

When he caught Rosie's eye over the rim of his glass he recognised her knowing expression. She'd seen him watching Milla. He looked away quickly. Rosie could think what she liked. Milla was a lovely girl—and he wasn't a monk—but if his sister was looking for a breakthrough in 'project Cormac' she'd be disappointed. He had no intention of letting Milla get close to him— he had nothing to offer except nightmares and bitterness and she deserved better than that.

He couldn't stay at the table if Rosie was going to be watching him. He hated that kind of attention.

Murmuring something about making a start on laying the dance floor in the marquee, he ignored Lily's protests and left the dining room.

CHAPTER FIVE

MILLA COULD TELL it was early by the quality of the silence. She yawned and rubbed her eyes. The palaver over her ankle and the verbal jousting during last night's dinner had exhausted her emotional reserves. She wondered what was going on between Cormac and his father—what had sent Cormac from the table in such a hurry. After he'd gone she'd been drawn into a discussion about wedding flowers for the marquee, and had soon been forced to make her own excuses for leaving the table.

Gingerly she moved her injured foot under the duvet before swinging her legs out of bed and testing it on the floor. Happy that she could put some weight on it, she pulled on her robe and then, with the aid of the stick Sam had given her, made her way quietly down to the kitchen.

She'd just made a pot of tea when the door opened and Cormac came in.

'Good morning.'

He looked fresh in his jeans and tee shirt. Caught in his steady gaze, she blushed. Her silk robe suddenly felt too loose and she tugged it around herself, knotting the belt firmly. 'Oh, good morning. I—I wasn't expecting to meet anyone...'

He glanced at her foot. 'How's the ankle?'

A trace of his scent reached her through the air and she remembered the day before, how it had felt to be held in his arms. 'It's a bit better, thanks. I managed the stairs, anyway.'

'Well, don't overdo it.' He pulled out a chair and motioned for her to sit down. 'You need to keep the weight off it.'

Milla lowered herself onto the chair and watched as he lifted two cups from the dresser. The skin at the back of his neck was golden, his hair neatly clipped. She wished she could stop noticing him in that way. It was unsettling—and pointless. After Dan, she wasn't interested in falling for anyone else. She'd only find more rejection, more hurt. If she could just get away from Calcarron House and be on her own again, then everything would be all right.

He put a mug of tea in front of her. 'I thought I'd make an early start; go up to the bothy to look at the water pipe, although I'm not sure when you'll be able—'

Her pulse quickened—this was her ticket to freedom. 'Please take me with you!'

His brow furrowed. 'You're in no state to go back—'

'I'll be fine. Really. I can't stay here.' It was hard to keep the emotion out of her voice. 'You've all been so kind, but I need to be at the bothy—I need to be on my own. Can't you understand? Even with my own room here I'm still in a house full of people—and there's all this wedding stuff going on... I mean, your family doesn't need to be worrying about me as well. Please, Cor...'

'I don't think—'

She clutched at desperate straws. 'Just for this morning, then...like a trial period...while you fix the water. If I can't manage I'll be honest about it and I'll come back, but, please, let me try.'

Cormac sighed and folded his arms. 'All right, but I'm not taking your stuff back because I don't think you're ready to manage on your own. If you prove me wrong, then I'll bring your bag up later. Deal?'

She resisted the urge to hobble across the room and hug him. 'Deal. You've no idea how happy I am.'

His eyes held the suggestion of a smile. 'If I were you I'd drink that tea quickly and get ready to go, because I'm certain that if anyone finds out what we're planning there'll be an uproar. I'll fill some bottles of water to take with us.'

At Calcarron, she'd let Cormac help her into the Jeep, but at Strathburn she was determined to show her independence from the outset, and insisted on making her own way to the bothy door. Inside, she was instantly claimed by the sense of peace and belonging she'd felt when she'd first arrived, and she found herself smiling as she hobbled into the studio.

When Cormac came in a few moments later he had that strange, hazy look in his eyes which she found so disconcerting.

'I've put the water bottles on the counter in the kitchen, in case you want to make coffee. I'll be up the hill if you need me.'

She pushed the hair away from her face and smiled. 'Thanks, but I'll be doing my best not to need you—otherwise you'll never believe that I can manage on my own.'

His eyes lingered on hers for a moment and then he smiled briefly. 'Right, I'd better get on, then.' He took a backward step, then turned and disappeared through the door.

She was relieved when he'd gone. Perhaps it was the light in the studio which mesmerised her, giving his eyes that faraway look that turned her inside out.

She opened her folder of urban portraits and spread them out on the bench, but the images quickly blurred. She shook herself and picked up each photograph in turn. Was she imagining it, that feeling that maybe Cormac liked her? Or was it wishful thinking—a silly fantasy? She sighed. This was all Dan's fault. He'd made her feel so unlovable that the idea of being liked by someone else—even Cormac—was compelling. That was it! That would explain all these feelings she was having.

She selected a photograph and put the others aside. Of course Cormac *was* very attractive and capable—and they both liked Monty Python—but he was also rather aloof. It had been quite easy to persuade him to bring her back to the bothy, so he obviously wasn't that keen to have her around at the house.

As she set her pencils and paper out on the bench, she felt clearer in her head. She'd been imagining things about Cormac that weren't real, all to boost her own bruised ego. Cormac had no interest in her and she had no interest in him. If she could convince him that she'd be perfectly fine at the bothy by herself she'd be free, and wouldn't have to endure another family dinner filled with wedding talk.

* * *

Scudding grey-white clouds rolled across the blue sky as Cormac climbed upwards, following the pipe towards the water tank. He'd fix the water today, no matter how long it took, because then Milla would be able to stay at the bothy. It was what she wanted and it was what he wanted too.

An image filled his head—tousled hair framing her perfect face, the swell of her breasts against the blue silk robe as she'd cinched it around her slender waist. She was an unwelcome distraction and, no matter how high he built his fences, she kept finding a way over them.

The infinite depths of her eyes…the curve of her cheek…her mouth…her smile. He'd thought he was immune until yesterday, when he'd carried her back to the house. With her arms around his neck and her head against his she'd destroyed his barricade and planted a seed of longing which was now growing and twisting inside him like a vine.

He didn't want to feel like this. Yearning for something he couldn't have. It would be so easy to fall in love with Milla, but he couldn't let it happen. She deserved a hero, and he was a mess. He couldn't open up, he was cynical and moody, and he couldn't sleep for the nightmares which made him judder and sweat.

At least she seemed oblivious to the effect she was having on him. Her ignorance was the only card he had left, and he had every intention of keeping it close to his chest.

He reached the tank and plunged his hand into the icy water to check the filter. Battling his attraction to Milla wasn't the only thing he had on his mind. Last night his father had made an unsubtle allusion to *family* being 'hands-on' at Calcarron. There were new ideas for diversification on the estate, and of course he was interested, but he wasn't ready to leave the army. He had to prove to himself that he could go back into the field, and until he'd done that he'd be no use to his father.

He found a tuft of sheep's wool clogging the pipe near a joint halfway down the hill—it must have been sucked into the outlet through the damaged filter he'd found in the tank. He'd have to replace the filter with a new one, but for now, with the water flowing again, Milla would be able to stay on at Strathburn and that would make them both happy.

He'd go and tell her, then go back to Calcarron.

When he entered the bothy he was greeted by an intoxicating aroma of brewing coffee. 'Hi! Milla?'

She appeared in the studio doorway wearing

a vest top, her cardigan knotted loosely around her hips.

He ran a hand across his forehead and concentrated on her eyes. 'The water's fixed. If you think you'll be okay, I'll leave you to it.'

'That's fantastic news.' She smiled hesitantly. 'I made coffee. Would you like some?' Strands of hair curled at the side of her neck where they'd broken free from her chignon and she pushed them away carelessly.

In his head he'd definitely been thinking no to coffee, but what came out of his mouth was, 'Yes, coffee would be great!'

She limped over to the cafetière, poured two mugs and handed them to him. 'Shall we go outside? It's so warm in the studio that I could use some fresh air.'

She picked up a sketchbook from the counter and went ahead of him onto the deck. He watched her ribcage rise as she breathed in the cool air, saw tiny goosebumps springing to life on her smooth arms and wondered why he'd agreed to stay. He could be halfway back to Calcarron by now.

She parked herself on the edge of the hammock and took the mug he handed to her. An uneasy light played across her eyes and he turned away, concentrating on the view as he sipped his coffee. 'So…how's the work coming along?'

Her sigh was heavy. 'To be honest, I'm having a bit of a meltdown.'

He shot her a curious glance. She'd seemed so confident about her work when she'd been talking about it at dinner.

'You see, I… I lost my way for a while with the work I was doing, and my tutor suggested that I try something different.' She sipped her coffee slowly. 'At the time it seemed like good advice, but now I'm not so sure. I'm working on a series of urban portraits, but I'm struggling with it because in truth I'm a country girl. I've got this exhibition coming up, and the pressure of that is making things worse.'

Her confessional tone was snagging his curiosity, but he couldn't allow himself to be interested.

He drained his mug. 'I'm sorry about that. I'll get out of your way and let you concentrate.'

'No! Please wait.'

The catch in her voice pulled him up short.

'I want to show you something—will you come and sit for a minute?'

He didn't want to sit beside her, but she'd picked up her sketchpad and she was gazing at him with expectant eyes. He set down his mug and joined her on the hammock.

She opened the book to a view he recognised straight away: Calcarron House. Perfectly proportioned, perfectly situated, with the hills rising behind and above a spectacular sky pierced by a shaft of sunlight. It was a simple pencil sketch, but it took his breath away.

He lifted his eyes to hers. 'This is wonderful, Milla. Stunning.'

She smiled. 'Yesterday I made five sketches in two hours, and I never noticed the time passing because I loved what I was doing. When my tutor turned me towards portraiture it was because...' She fell silent for a moment. 'Anyway, he was wrong. I'm a landscape artist. It's what I've always been. I need scenery and grand views, tones and textures.' She pinned him with a wide green gaze. 'The trouble is, I can't get anywhere with a twisted ankle...'

Cormac felt something like the start-up lurch of a runaway train. Her hand was on his arm, lustrous eyes locked on his, and he knew he'd have to stamp on the brakes immediately.

He lifted her hand from his arm and rose to his feet. 'No way! I'm not taking you on some crazy art safari. You can barely walk, and I've got a dance floor to lay in the marquee.'

'Please, Cor. Just two hours of your time is all I'm asking. If you take me to some good places

I'll sketch quickly, and then I promise I'll stay out of your way for the rest of my time here.'

He stared at her in disbelief. She was actually serious. 'No! I don't have the time and it'll make your ankle worse.'

Her eyes held him fast. 'It won't—if you get me to the right spots I'll hardly have to walk at all… What do I have to do to persuade you?'

'You *won't* persuade me.'

He watched as she fingered her sketchbook, then he saw a smile slowly lighting up her face.

'You like this sketch of Calcarron House, don't you? What about if I scale this up into a painting? You could keep it for yourself, or maybe Rosie would like it as a wedding present…'

A painting of Calcarron House for Rosie would be the perfect wedding gift. There was no way he could refuse her now. She'd played the ace and won.

Milla gave in to the jolting motion of the four-by-four as they progressed along the track. Cormac seemed to know the depth of every rut, handling the vehicle with a skill that she felt sure her father would admire. His eyes were trained on the view ahead and there was something about the firmness of his jaw which betrayed—what? Irritation?

Not once had he looked at her, and she couldn't blame him. She'd manipulated him shamelessly, but she'd had no choice. She hadn't lied when she'd told him she was in a panic. The portraits weren't working. She had to change course quickly if she had any hope of completing her exhibition pieces, and Cormac was the only one who could help her do it.

Secretly she studied his hands on the wheel. Tanned, capable hands, with neatly trimmed nails. The same hands that had gently examined her injuries before lifting her into strong arms.

His body against hers had felt hard and warm, the scent of his skin inexplicably intoxicating. She'd breathed him in as he walked, clenching her hands ever tighter to stop herself from sliding her fingers over the curve of his bicep and caressing the smooth skin at the back of his neck.

She lifted her eyes to his face. His lips were pressed together in concentration and she moistened her own, wondering for a moment how those lips would feel against hers. Gentle, tender, urgent, perhaps... The thought of it made her dizzy.

What was happening to her? In the studio she'd almost convinced herself that she had no interest in him, yet here she was again, fantasising. What was it about Cormac Buchanan that moved her? He'd never flirted with her—in fact he was locked down so tight she was surprised he could even breathe. Nonetheless, something about his proximity was making her insides churn, and as he brought the vehicle to a halt she reached for the door handle with relief.

In front of her stretched a vaguely familiar plateau dominated by five standing stones. The distant mountains had faded to a purple haze, and above them a multitude of dramatic cloud formations shifted through the sky. As the breeze whipped at her cheeks Milla could almost hear the chanting voices of an ancient ritual being carried on the wind and she felt her spirit reaching out.

'It's strange. I feel like I've been here before.'

His voice came to her from behind. 'My grandfather liked painting this scene...'

'Of course!' She turned to face him. 'The painting in my room—this place is its inspiration.'

He nodded, and for a few moments their eyes locked across the silence—until Milla noticed the sound of the wind rustling through the grass. She broke away from his gaze and looked up, saw a buzzard wheeling overhead, its wing-tips tilting as it patrolled the sky, and she wondered how Cormac could bear to leave such wild beauty.

'Do you miss this when you're away?'

'Yes.'

She felt her brow creasing. 'Just "yes"…?'

He nodded and looked away. 'Too many stories, too little time. We're on the clock, remember?'

His cool detachment no longer bothered her. She could see that he used it like a weapon, and she wondered about it, but then she remembered that *he* was none of her business.

She smiled. 'Okay, well, I'd like to go that way to get a better angle.' She pointed to a narrow track through the heather.

He picked up her bag and walked ahead.

She'd put on walking boots to cradle her ankle, but it wasn't easy going, even with the stick, and before long she was consumed with irritation and dismay.

At the foot of a low rise he stood waiting for her. 'This is a bad idea, Milla. You're going to make your ankle worse if you go any further.'

He was right, even though it hurt her to admit it. She eased herself onto a boulder and tried not to sound petulant. 'I'll just have to stay here, then. Can I have my bag, please?'

He put it into her hands and stepped back. 'I'll make myself scarce for a while, if you're all right on your own.'

She nodded, forcing back her tears of frustration. 'I'm fine, yes...please, just go.'

She watched him striding away up the rise and felt a pang of envy. He was heading for the spot with the best view and she couldn't get there. She yanked open the zip of her bag and pulled out her sketchpad. She'd just have to make the best of where she was.

She toyed with an abstract treatment and then, as her pencil began to fly over the paper, she lost herself in the world she was creating.

From his vantage point on the hillside Cormac watched her. He'd known that she would struggle to walk along the rough path, but he admired her spirit. At least she seemed to be absorbed now, so perhaps she was happy.

He turned his attention to the view, but when he realised that he was scanning the stones for signs of the enemy he dropped his head into his hands. There was no enemy here—only memories.

He forced himself to look up again and let himself remember how much Duncan had loved this place. He'd been fascinated by the stones, and by the ancients who'd placed them here. When they were children they'd come with picnics; when they were teenagers they'd come with hip flasks of whisky, secretly filled from his father's decanter.

He smiled at the memory, the way the whisky had loosened their tongues, but they'd always told each other everything anyway. It was how he'd known what Duncan wanted…

The last time he'd been here he'd been with Duncan's widow, Emma, to scatter his friend's ashes. When Milla had asked him if he missed the estate he hadn't known what to say. He missed it all the time, but it was different for him now, and he couldn't tell her about that.

'This is such a peaceful place, Cor. There's a calm, spiritual vibe… When my foot's better I'm coming back. I want to touch the stones, and I want to see the view from where you were.'

'Good idea.'

Her mood had softened and her affinity for the stones touched him, seemed to release some of the pressure in his head.

He smiled. 'Ready to go?'

'Sure.'

She wriggled off the boulder, but as her feet touched the ground she stumbled and he lunged to steady her. 'Are you okay?'

'Yes, I'm fine…'

Her bare arms felt cool beneath his fingers.

When she moistened her lips he felt himself drifting, imagining how they would feel against his.

When he realised he was still holding her he released her quickly. 'We should get going.'

She smiled. 'Lead the way, Commander. I'll bring up the rear—very slowly.'

She wasn't wrong. As she hobbled back to the vehicle he could tell that her ankle was hurting, and by the time he'd settled her into the passenger seat he'd made a decision.

It didn't take her long to notice that he was retracing their route to the bothy.

'Why are you going back this way? It's too soon.'

He pulled over. 'You're tired.'

'No, I'm not. I'm fine.'

'You're not fine, but you're too stubborn to admit it. I'm taking you back.' He reached for the gears.

'No!' Her eyes gleamed with tears. 'Okay, I give in—my ankle *is* hurting—but I can tough it out for the sake of my work. You're a soldier—don't tell me you don't get it. Haven't you ever had to push on through your pain?'

She knew exactly how to touch a nerve.

'Cor, please—don't take me back yet. I need this.'

In her eyes he saw all her fragility and determination laid bare, and something else that skewed his senses.

He sighed. 'Okay, you win. There's a place I know—I'll show it to you—and after that I'm calling time. You should be resting that foot, not clambering up mountains.'

'But I need—'

'You need to rest, otherwise you'll have to come back to the house—and I know you don't want to do that, right?'

He could see her calculating just how far she could push him and he suppressed a smile.

She capitulated. 'Okay. Show me the place you know and we'll call it a day.'

'Sensible decision. Now, you might want to hold on tight—where we're going involves a little off-road climbing.'

He pulled away, then turned off the track and inched the four-by-four up the hillside, trying not to laugh at the way she was hanging onto the door grip.

She threw him a glance. 'You weren't wrong about the climb. No! Don't look at me when I'm talking to you. Just keep your eyes on the non-existent track.'

He laughed. 'I know what I'm doing. You're perfectly safe.'

She pressed herself back into the seat. 'It's funny you should say that, because I was just thinking to myself how *perfectly safe* I was feeling.'

'Don't you trust me?'

It suddenly occurred to Cormac that he was having fun. He angled the Jeep so that it would slide back a couple of inches and threw her a panicked look. 'Oh, no! I'm losing control… prepare to bail.'

She squealed. 'I wasn't born yesterday, Cormac Buchanan. I know you did that on purpose.' She was laughing now. 'Will you stop all your fooling and get us to the top before I have a stupid heart attack?'

She was still laughing when he pulled on the handbrake. 'Now, *there's* a view: Loch Calcarron and mountains that go on for ever. It doesn't get any better than this.'

He hesitated for a moment, but the laughter they'd shared had lightened his spirits and suddenly he was happy to share something else with her.

'This is my favourite place in the world.'

He heard her catch her breath. 'This *is* the place—this is *definitely* the place.' She was unclipping her seat belt. 'I need to get out.'

'I thought we'd agreed? You've got to rest that ankle.'

He caught a glimmer of mischief in her eye.

'We did agree, and I'm not going back on it, but I need to take a proper look.'

When he arrived at her side she was reaching for her stick, but the thought of more hobbling was too much for him. 'Leave it. It'll be no good here, anyway. Take my hand.'

He detected a flicker of uncertainty in her eyes as she slipped her hand into his, and worried that his gesture was being misconstrued.

He decided that he needed to be breezier. 'So where are we going?'

She pointed to a place a short distance away. 'Over there—to that big boulder.'

'Okay, let's go.'

He led her through clumps of heather and carried her across the rocks in places where it was too awkward for her to walk. When he finally set her down he felt a sheen of perspiration between his shoulder blades. It wasn't the effort of lifting her that had heated his veins; it was the simple fact of her existence.

Milla pressed her palm into the boulder she was sitting on, trying to erase the invisible imprint of his hand around hers. As he'd driven them up the slope she'd finally seen that smile, like the smile in that photograph with his friend, and she couldn't get it out of her head. Nor the way he'd taken her hand, then lifted her across the rocks.

He'd been playful, pretending to lose his footing once or twice, and she'd laughed. That they could have fun together was a revelation, but it scared her too. He was letting his guard down by degrees, and a few degrees could change everything. Fantasising about a kiss was harmless enough, but she couldn't let herself really like him—couldn't allow herself to get close.

She'd been hurt before and she wouldn't let it happen again. More than ever she needed to lose herself in her work, leave no space for anything else.

Cormac's favourite place would be her new beginning. He was right—the view across the mountains was breathtaking—but from the moment she'd set eyes on this craggy backbone of granite she'd felt a surge of inspiration rushing through her blood. These rocks whispered to her so intimately that it felt like destiny.

The scrape of boots jolted her back to the moment. He set her bag down and she squinted up at him.

'Thanks for going back to get it.'

He frowned. 'I'd like to say it was a pleasure, but setting up camp here wasn't part of the agreement.'

She unzipped the bag and pulled out her sketchbook. 'I know you're cross, but I promise I won't be long. You brought me here, and I love it, so you should be pleased.'

He sat down and leaned against a boulder. 'I'll try to remember that when I'm explaining to Rosie why her dance floor isn't laid.'

He tipped his head back and closed his eyes against the sun's glare.

She gazed at his face for a moment, then opened her sketchbook. 'Rosie will forgive you when you give her a painting of Calcarron House as a wedding present.'

Milla drove her pencil over the paper, outlining shapes, shading crevices, scratching flicks for grass. She mixed colours in her head and made notes—greys and mauves, bright yellows fading to bleached golds, deeper greens and darker browns. She worked quickly, aware that Cormac's patience was running out.

When she finally lifted her eyes she was surprised to find him staring at her.

'What are you seeing in the rocks? I thought you wanted me to show you a view.'

'It *is* a view.'

'Hmm...but aren't the mountains and the loch more of a landscape? You said you painted landscapes.'

'I do paint landscapes. This *is* a landscape.' She turned towards the ridge. 'You asked me what I see... I see sanctuary—a place of safety where someone might hide or shelter. I see history—I feel the power of whatever it was that formed these rocks—and in the cracks and crevices I see the passage of time, the forces of erosion. There's a rich mosaic of texture and colour here which I can exaggerate into a bold abstract...'

'You see all that?'

She turned back to him and nodded. 'I do. What do you see?'

He rose to his feet and rubbed the back of his neck. 'I see rocks. We need to go.'

He extended his hand for her sketchbook, then helped her up.

She tried not to lean against him too much as he helped her back to the Jeep, but she couldn't resist having the last word.

'You can always see more if you want to. You just have to open your eyes a little wider, that's all.'

The truth was that Cormac understood about the rocks. He'd sought their sanctuary many times. A tower of granite at your back offered respite from looking over your shoulder, and such a view might convince you that a greater hand than yours was guiding your fate—at least it might if you had any faith left.

That Milla had found inspiration in his special place had annoyed him as much as it had pleased him, but if he was annoyed it was only because he was supposed to be elsewhere. There would be questions about his long absence, and he'd have to lie and say that the blockage in the pipe had taken longer to find than he'd expected.

He chose a gentler route for their descent, and soon re-joined the track which led to the bothy. In a clearing, he pulled over and let the vehicle idle.

'When you're on foot you can get to the ridge that way.' He pointed to a path which wound steeply upwards to a gap between two giant shards of granite. 'When you get to the top you'll recognise where we were.'

'Thanks.'

He slowed to steer them through a deep rut in the track. 'Don't get any ideas about going soon, though—it's quite a walk from the bothy and you're nowhere near fit for the distance.'

'No.'

He glanced at her. She was being uncharacteristically meek. 'You're quiet.'

'I'm a bit tired.'

'Sorry, I didn't catch that?'

She lifted an eyebrow. 'Very funny.'

At the bothy, he helped her out of the vehicle and walked her to the door. 'You definitely want to stay here?'

'Yes.'

Her eyes flickered with an emotion he couldn't read.

'I think that would be best… What I mean is that I really need to focus on my work.'

He felt drawn into her gaze and stepped back. 'I'll bring your stuff from the house later on— check that you're all right.' For some reason his hands felt superfluous and he shoved them into his pockets. 'Have you got food?'

Her lips curved into a smile. 'Yes, I have. Honestly, I'll be fine.'

He turned to leave, finding it harder than he thought it would be.

'Cormac!'

He spun round.

'Please thank your family for me. Can you explain—?'

'Of course. You're forgetting that my grand-father was an artist—they're used to it.'

She smiled. 'And thank *you* for everything. You've been very…'

'And you've also been very…' He grinned. 'I'll see you later.'

She laughed. 'Not if I see you first.'

CHAPTER SIX

CORMAC LOOKED AROUND the room in case he'd missed anything, but Milla had only used a few pages in one of his grandfather's sketchbooks. She'd left it open on the table. He stared at an unfinished sketch of a face. It had to be one of the urban portraits she'd talked about—the eyes certainly had a sad, brooding quality.

If she was having an artistic crisis then he could understand why she'd bribed him with the promise of a painting in return for a tour of the wilds, but he hadn't wanted to ask her what had thrown her off course. It was none of his business. *She* was none of his business—even if he kept having to remind himself of it.

He fingered the folder in his hands, then tucked it into the sketchbook and closed the cover. He'd take it up to the bothy; she might find it useful.

He looked up as Rosie came into the room with Milla's holdall and jacket.

'That was easy! She'd hardly unpacked a thing.'

'Well, she wasn't planning to stay.'

He reached for the bag, but Rosie put it down and fixed him with a wide, blue gaze.

'Hang on a sec. I want to talk to you.'

He heard a distant ringing of alarm bells. 'Oh?'

'Don't get defensive, okay, but last night at dinner I couldn't help noticing the way you were looking at Milla.'

'You're imagining—'

'No, I'm not. You're my brother. I can read you like a book.'

'For goodness' sake—'

'Stop interrupting. I'm trying to say something.'

He knew Rosie would never let him go until he'd heard her out. 'Okay. What?'

He folded his arms and watched her cross to the bookcase. She picked up a silver frame he recognised.

'I love this photo of you and Duncan. You look so happy.'

He felt his chest tighten. 'And your point is?'

She put the frame back. 'I want you to be happy again, more than anything. I want my brother back—not this shadow you've become. Milla's a sweet girl, but she seems…'

'What?'

'Uptight. Fragile. I can't put my finger on it, but I'm wondering if this is the kind of girl you should be falling for—'

Cormac felt a stab of irritation. 'Who says I'm "falling" for her? I'm not interested in attachments—you know that. If I was looking at her it's because she's pretty, that's all.' He picked up the holdall and walked to the door. 'I need to drop off her stuff. I'll see you later.'

He set off for Strathburn, berating himself for flying off the handle. Rosie hadn't meant any harm—she was only concerned about him. They all were. He sighed. He never used to be so volatile. It was the legacy of Afghanistan, and one of the reasons he was now chained to a desk at Chatham.

When Rosie had called him a shadow, she was right. He was a hollow shell filled with darkness.

Milla folded her arms and inspected her work. Around her, the floor was littered with charcoal sketches—studies of outlines and textures, rock formations and dramatic skies. Charcoal wasn't her usual medium, but it felt right for these studies—bold, dark strokes for the wild and rugged landscape that was Cormac's favourite place.

She'd just started a new sketch when a sharp knocking sound startled her, and then she remembered Cormac's promise to come back with her things. She tidied her hair with her hands, then limped out of the studio, but he'd already opened the door and was standing in the threshold. At the sight of him she felt a familiar thrill tingling in her veins and an unwelcome rush of heat in her cheeks.

To hide it she launched an offensive. 'You frightened the life out of me creeping in like that. Were you in Black Ops, by any chance?'

His mouth twisted into a wry smile. 'I did knock. As for Black Ops—I could ask you the same thing.' She must have looked perplexed because he added, 'You might want to look in a mirror...'

She looked down at her oily hands, then noticed the smudges on her vest. 'I'm covered in charcoal, aren't I?'

His eyebrows lifted. 'You could say that.' He took a few steps towards her and motioned to the bag in his hand. 'I've brought your stuff and there's a sketchbook in the car...it's the one you were using in the studio. I didn't know if you'd want it or not...'

She felt a little jolt of dismay. The last thing she remembered drawing was... 'Did you look inside at all?'

'It was lying open. I saw a pair of sad eyes and then it all got too much for me.'

It had only been a partial sketch, and there was every chance he hadn't recognised himself, but she wasn't sure. When she felt his hand on her shoulder she came back to herself and saw that he was smiling at her.

'Milla, I'm teasing.'

The warmth of his fingers on her skin and the way he was looking at her threw her off balance. Perhaps he felt it too, because he dropped his hand to his side and the spell was broken.

She stepped back. 'You might be teasing, but you're right about the sad eyes. I'm glad I've gone back to landscapes.' She smiled and tried to sound casual. 'Even so, I'd like to keep the book, if that's okay. I'll go and clean up. Be careful where you walk if you go into the studio—there's work everywhere.'

She confronted her reflection in the bathroom mirror and laughed. Cormac's reaction had been typically understated. She was so smudged with black that she did indeed resemble a marine on a covert mission. A wash in the tiny sink wouldn't cut it, so she showered quickly and put on clean jeans and a top. She brushed out her hair and tried to draw it up into messy bun, but for some reason she was all fingers and thumbs.

She could still feel the warmth of his hand on

her shoulder and it was sapping her concentration. The way he'd looked at her, that soft light in his eyes... She didn't want to feel these giddy butterflies cavorting around in her stomach.

She stared at herself and took a steadying breath, then forced her fingers to work her hair into the clip. She needed to get her feelings about Cormac into perspective. They'd had a nice morning together. He'd seemed friendlier than before, less starchy. He'd opened up a bit, so she'd warmed to him, but it didn't mean anything except that maybe they were friends now.

She tucked a stray lock of hair behind her ear and put a fresh plaster over the cut on her hand. A minor injury—he must have seen so much worse. Yet again, she wondered what tragedy could have so altered him that the local villagers would throw its bones into casual conversation. Sam had said that Cormac had been in Afghanistan. That was bound to change a person. But at the end of the day it wasn't any of her business. She should go and thank him for bringing her things back.

She found him in the studio, inspecting her work. He looked up as she entered and for a second she saw it again, that cloudy look in his eyes.

'These are really good, Milla.'

'Thanks, but they're only studies...' She felt a

strange skittering sensation in her veins, a sudden dryness in her mouth. With difficulty, she swallowed. 'The final pieces will be oil on canvas.'

He walked around the sketches carefully. 'Well, I think these work on their own merits.' He looked up and smiled. 'Just my opinion.'

'Thanks.' She didn't understand why his smile was making her blush, but the way he was looking at her was very disconcerting.

He glanced at her foot. 'How's it feeling?'

She looked down and shrugged. 'I haven't noticed it, to be honest, but then again I don't notice much when I'm working. I suppose it's aching a bit; I've been on it all afternoon.'

His eyes narrowed. 'It's not the afternoon. It's after seven.'

'You're joking—right?'

'I'm not!' He frowned. 'Have you eaten anything since I left?'

She was floundering now. 'No. I was going to, but…'

His lips straightened into a line of exasperation. 'You're just like my grandfather. He'd forget everything when he was painting. You need to eat, and you need to rest. Your ankle won't mend like this.'

'I know, but I'm feeling so pressured about this exhibition. It's making me—'

'Foolish! That's the word you're looking for.'

His irritation seemed disproportionate to the crime and Milla bristled with indignation. 'And you're never foolish, I suppose?'

He stared at her for a moment and then the storm in his eyes passed. 'I'm not saying that, but if you're staying here you need to take care of yourself. That was the deal, remember?' Unexpectedly, he broke into a smile. 'Do you have a box of cornflakes?'

She squeezed her eyes shut and laughed. 'I don't know why I even told you that—and, actually, no, I don't. I was going to shop properly the day after I arrived but then I came to the house...'

He studied her for a moment. 'Well, I won't have you starving to death on my watch. I'm taking you for dinner.' He must have read her thoughts because he added: 'Don't worry. I'm not taking you to the house. I have somewhere else in mind.'

Was this a date or was he simply looking after her? Milla was confused. She glanced at him sideways. He looked relaxed—relaxed in the way he would be if he was heading out for a bite to eat with a friend. So—not a date, then, which was perfect.

She felt the evening sunlight playing across her face as he drove them through a winding glen and she closed her eyes. Why hadn't she said no? She could have told him she had some-thing in the fridge—she needn't have told him it was only yoghurt. She didn't understand her-self. She'd just gone along with his idea and now it was too late to change her mind.

She fingered the catch on her bag, and then remembered how her mother used to tell her not to fidget, so she clasped her hands together and tried to focus on the view.

They'd emerged from the glen into a village, quaint, with narrow streets, neatly painted cot-tages and bright window boxes. Rows of colour-ful bunting flapped in the breeze and she found herself smiling.

Cormac caught her eye. 'The bunting's up for a local food festival—it makes the place look pretty for the tourists.'

She laughed. 'Well, speaking as a tourist, I'd say it's working.'

After a steep, twisting descent, the road opened out onto a waterfront. Cormac pulled over in front of a broad deck strung with light-bulbs and switched off the engine. 'This is the Pier Smokehouse—it serves *the* best smoked seafood in Scotland. The view's pretty good too.'

Milla gazed past the deck to the loch beyond. 'It's lovely… But this can't be Loch Calcarron?'

'You're right.' He unclipped his seat belt. 'The

glen we came through connects Calcarron to Collis—this is Loch Collis—it's a sea loch.' He smiled. 'Let's go.'

He helped her down from the four-by-four, his hand firm at her elbow. It was a simple courtesy, but in the context of this outing the lines felt blurry and yet again Milla wondered why she'd agreed to let him take her for dinner.

He released her and stepped back. 'You can use my arm, or I'll get your stick…'

Entering the restaurant on Cormac's arm would be muddying the waters way too much; this non-date was already confusing.

She smiled. 'I'll go under my own steam, if you don't mind.'

'Why should I mind?'

He handed her the stick, then stepped aside to let her go through the timber arch which marked the way onto the decking.

He fell in beside her, adjusting his pace to hers. 'Strictly speaking, it's more of a landing stage than a pier, but it's a great location for a restaurant. In high season it's mobbed.'

Now that she was through the arch she could see the old smokehouse more clearly. It was a narrow building of weathered timber, its rusticity offset by crisp modern signage and tasteful metal planters filled with decorative grasses. Through the windows she could see red-checked tablecloths and winking tea lights. It was perfect—the kind of place that would have appealed to her if this had been a date. Which, she reminded herself, it wasn't.

Inside, it was busy. She thought they'd have to wait, but Cormac seemed to know the owner and within moments they'd been shown to a corner table next to the window. As the waiter fussed around them, pouring glasses of iced water, she looked at Cormac and he caught her looking and smiled. She smiled back, and then, for something to do, slipped off her cardigan and arranged it over the back of her chair.

Did this whole thing feel as strange to him as it did to her?

When the waiter came back and handed her a tall menu she was relieved. She held it in front of her face and scanned the room. There was no getting away from it; this was a very romantic restaurant and she absolutely had to stop the butterflies racing around in her stomach.

When she'd composed herself, she lowered her menu slightly and risked a glance across the table. The low sun shining through the window bathed his skin in golden light, illuminating the shards of amber in his irises as he scanned the menu. Absently he drew his thumb across his lower lip and Milla's insides churned.

Perhaps he heard the catch in her breath because he looked up, caught her in his enquiring gaze. She smiled quickly and looked down again, pretending to study the menu.

'Have you chosen?'

'I—I thought I'd let you recommend something.' She couldn't tell him she hadn't read a word.

'Okay…sea cucumber or hot smoked salmon?'

She grinned, thankful for his easy humour. 'Hmm…the sea cucumber sounds tempting, but I think I'll take my chances with the salmon.'

The waiter took their order and disappeared. Cormac topped up their water glasses while she gazed across the loch, wondering what on earth they were going to talk about. Jolting through the countryside together looking for landscapes to draw was one thing; facing each other across a table in a candlelit restaurant was quite another.

'So, is this better than cornflakes?'

He was looking at her softly, a flicker of uncertainty in his eyes. Maybe he was feeling it too, the strangeness.

She smiled. 'Definitely better than cornflakes—but I'm worried that your family will miss you at dinner.'

He sipped his water. 'It'll be fine. You're not the only one who doesn't want to listen to the ins and outs of table plans and hand-tied bouquets.'

'I'm impressed that you even know the terminology.' She felt her cheeks colouring and looked down at her glass. 'I find the whole thing—'

'I know.'

He was looking at her intently, and the curiosity in his eyes only increased her agitation. She didn't want to talk about her past, but on the other hand, if he knew, he'd be a more effective ally against further invitations to the house.

She moistened her lips. 'You want to know why, don't you?'

He shook his head. 'It's none of my business.'

She shifted her gaze to the loch. It didn't matter any more anyway—nothing she could tell him would change anything. 'I was engaged, planning my own wedding, when my fiancé broke it off.'

'I'm sorry, Milla. That's really tough.'

The kindness in his voice almost brought tears to her eyes but she didn't care. Now that she'd started, she wanted him to know everything. 'Dan was working away in Berlin—he's still there, actually—and he met someone else. Someone he loved more than me.'

Cormac sat in silence. She managed a smile. 'Maybe it was a good thing. What I mean is that at least it happened before we were married.'

'Maybe—but pain is pain, whenever it comes.'

She could see it again, a depth of sadness in

his eyes which made her want to ask him… But she couldn't.

She took a sip of water from her glass. 'The break-up knocked me for six, affected my work—everything, really. It's why I'm here. My tutor suggested it—he said being here would help.'

Cormac's mouth twisted into a wry smile. 'I can see it's been a big help—no water at the bothy, a wrenched ankle and a serious case of wedding fever. If I'd known all this before—'

'It wouldn't have made any difference. You couldn't have stopped any of it happening.'

He was looking at her in that intense way of his and she felt the familiar dizzying spiral of awareness. She was glad when the waiter arrived with their order.

As they ate the sun slipped lower and the golden ambience of the interior intensified. With its waterside location and delicious food, Milla decided that the Pier Smokehouse could easily hold its own against any London restaurant, and as she put down her dessert spoon she realised that telling Cormac about her broken engagement had lightened her spirits somehow.

She caught his eye. 'It was nice of you to bring me here.'

He smiled. 'I could hardly let you starve, and I knew you wouldn't want to have dinner with my family again.'

'Your family is lovely—'

'I know—but things are hectic right now.'

She fiddled with her napkin, then smiled. 'How *did* you know the terminology for table plans and hand-tied bouquets?'

It had been a light-hearted question, so she was surprised to see a fleeting pain in his eyes.

He looked for the waiter, gestured for the bill, then turned to meet her gaze. 'I was best man for a friend. I must have absorbed more than I thought.'

His smile didn't quite reach his eyes, and as they stood up to leave Milla couldn't help thinking that she'd touched a nerve.

Cormac pulled on the handbrake and switched off the engine. He wondered what had made him say it. *'I was best man for a friend.'* He could have said anything at all—he could have said that he only knew wedding jargon because of Rosie—but instead he'd dipped his toe in the waters of intimacy and frightened himself.

Maybe it was because Milla had told him about her broken engagement—some subconscious part of him had wanted to open up too, tell her about Duncan. But he'd faltered at the last moment, and he knew that she was wondering why he'd been so quiet on drive back.

She started to move and he touched her shoulder. 'Sit tight. I'll help you to the door and see you safely inside.'

He felt her eyes on his. 'Thank you.'

Perhaps taking her out for dinner had been a mistake. When he'd brought up her bag nothing could have been further from his mind, but somehow events had overtaken him and now he was adrift, unsure of how to get things back to the way they were before.

As he unclipped his seat belt he felt grateful for the darkness, grateful that she couldn't see his face.

Inside the bothy he switched on the lamps for her and wondered how he was going to take his leave. It ought to be straightforward, but she was looking at him with that little crease in her forehead, as if she was trying to work something out.

He pushed a hand through his hair. 'I'll check the water filters before I go, okay?'

She smiled softly. 'Thanks, but I don't want to keep you. You've already done enough for me today.'

'It's no trouble; the cupboard's just through the back. It'll only take a second.'

When he returned she was holding the folder he'd slipped into her sketchbook and her face was lovely with smiles. 'I just found these photographs hidden in the sketchbook.' She took a step closer. 'You took them for me...thank you. It was kind of you.'

Her smile warmed him and he suddenly felt better. 'You couldn't manage the climb... I could see how frustrated you were.'

She held his gaze, then glanced at her foot. 'At least it's temporary—when this gets better there'll be no stopping me.'

The light in her eyes was mesmerising, and he swallowed. 'I'd better be going.'

She nodded. 'I'll show you out.'

On the deck, she lifted her face to the sky. 'So many stars; they never look as bright as this in London...'

'Because of the light pollution.' He tipped his head back. 'Desert stars look amazing too...'

'Oh, my!' She turned to look at him. 'Did you see that...?'

'I don't know...what did you see?'

'A green flash.' She threw him a playful glance. 'I'm thinking maybe it's the Martians landing...'

There was something irresistible about her turn of phrase and he found himself laughing. 'I'm sorry to disappoint you, but it's probably the Northern Lights starting—the Aurora Borealis— you should stay out here. You wouldn't want to miss it.'

The breeze lifted slightly and he noticed her pulling her cardigan tighter.

'There'd be nothing disappointing about seeing the Northern Lights. I've never seen them before…'

He wished he could stop noticing that little quirk of her mouth, the milky hollow at the base of her throat.

'But it would be nice to have company. Will you stay for a little while?'

She held him in her gaze and he felt his shoulders stiffen with momentary indecision. He knew he should go, but that awkwardness between them had gone, so perhaps there'd be no harm in staying to watch the lights with her, since it was her first time.

He licked his lips. 'Sure. Why not.'

She brightened. 'Would you like a drink? I've got whiskey—it's Irish, of course, but I won't tell anyone.'

'Irish sounds perfect to me.' He smiled. 'Tell me where it is and I'll get it.'

'Sláinte!'

She grinned. *'Sláinte chugat!'*

He swallowed a mouthful from his glass, felt the heat of it in his throat. He dropped down onto the deck, leaned against the plate-glass window and looked up, searching the sky as he weighed up safe topics of conversation.

'So, where's home?'

She was sitting on the hammock, wrapped in the blanket he'd brought out for her.

'Galway. My family's still there, but I've been in London for quite a while. What about you? Where are you based?'

He cursed silently. He didn't want to talk about the army, but it was too late now. He rolled the tumbler between his hands. 'Chatham. It's HQ for the Royal Engineers.'

'Do you like it there?'

He picked at a loose thread on his jeans. 'Not really.'

'So why—?'

She was unstoppable. 'I thought you wanted to watch the lights…'

'I can watch the lights and talk at the same time—it's called multi-tasking. Besides, you're the one who started the conversation.'

He sighed. 'I'm at Chatham because my tour came to an end.'

'Your *tour*?'

Was she being disingenuous? He glanced at her face; she looked innocent enough. 'Tour of duty. We get posted overseas for a period, and then we come back to base.'

'And you prefer being away?'

He pictured his desk at HQ, heaped with paper. 'Of course. That's where we do the real work. It's where we can make a difference.'

'So, where have you been on tour?'

A knot tightened in his stomach. He needed to distract her. 'You make me sound like a rock star.'

She sipped her whiskey and coughed it down, laughing. 'Well, it could happen. James Blunt was a soldier and now he *is* a rock star, so there's hope for you if you want a change of career. Obviously you'd have to be able to sing—'

He turned to look at her. 'You literally can't turn it off, can you? Words tumble out of your mouth and—'

'And what?'

'I don't know… You're funny.'

'In a good way, I hope?'

'Mostly good…' He felt a slow smile tugging at his lips, wondering what she'd make of that.

'Mostly?' She shrugged. 'Well, even professional comedians aren't funny all the time… Anyway, you were about to tell me about where you've been on your tours of duty…'

He gritted his teeth—she wasn't going to be distracted after all. 'The Balkans, Iraq… Afghanistan.'

'And where are you going next?'

A cold fist closed around his heart. He

watched the lights shimmering in the sky above. Next. There was no next for him—not until he'd been reassessed.

He struggled to make his voice sound casual as he rose to his feet. 'I haven't been assigned yet. I'm going to get a glass of water. Do you want one?'

In the kitchen he filled two glasses from the tap. Maybe the alcohol was fuelling her open curiosity, but he couldn't talk about Afghanistan, or his desk job, or about his future. He knew he ought to go. She kept asking him questions he didn't want to answer, and when she wasn't doing that she was just being herself. Her beautiful, bewitching self.

Back outside, he handed her a glass of water and watched the lights pulsing across the sky. He could feel the weight of her eyes on him and he wondered what was going through her mind, what she was seeing. He had a sudden curiosity about the kind of man she would be attracted to.

'Was your fiancé an artist too?'

She looked momentarily stunned, then she rallied. 'Yes, he was, but you know I don't want to talk about Daniel.'

'I'm sorry. That was clumsy of me—'

She tugged at the blanket. 'You don't have to be sorry. I'm over him—I just need a sticking plaster for my wounded pride.'

'That sounds like bravado to me.'

She laughed. 'What doesn't kill you makes you stronger.'

Her words sounded hollow to him, but he smiled anyway.

She swung off the hammock and limped to his side. 'You know, you're different from how you were when we first met.'

'Different?'

'Not so standoffish.'

'Standoffish?' He rubbed the back of his neck. 'Well, maybe it's because you've stopped being so spikey.'

It was her turn to look surprised. 'Spikey? Is that what you thought of me?'

He felt a smile creasing his cheeks. 'You came out with all guns blazing—I was only trying to help you change your wheel.'

He heard the laughter in her voice. 'Well, you didn't even introduce yourself. You were so aloof...you provoked me.'

He remembered the scene at the roadside— the wheel brace lying next to the punctured tyre, the jack close by. 'I'm sorry I didn't introduce myself. I was too busy trying not to step on your evidently capable toes.' He shrugged. 'I'll admit I'm not much good at small talk, but I listen, and I notice things.'

'Such as?'

'The Aurora. You really should look up.'

The lights were in full spate now—glowing curtains of emerald-green, pulsing and shimmering. Time stretched and for a moment it felt to Cormac as if they were the only two people on earth.

When she finally spoke, he heard a catch in her voice.

'It's beautiful, Cor, don't you think?'

She kept calling him 'Cor', and it sounded sweet from her mouth. He looked at her face, at the tiny lines wrinkling her forehead as she gazed at the sky, the smile playing on her lips. She was luminous, and the urge to touch her was overwhelming.

His voice emerged as a whisper. 'Amazing.'

She seemed to sense that he wasn't looking at the sky and turned to meet his gaze. 'You *were* talking about the lights, right…?'

He watched the reflections dancing in her eyes and hesitated. 'I was talking about the view.' He didn't know why he'd laid himself bare like that, but he saw an answering glimmer in her eyes that felt like an invitation.

Slowly, he lifted a hand to her cheek, traced the line of her jaw with his fingers, and then, as another flash lit the sky over their heads, he stepped closer. He couldn't stop himself now. With infinite slowness he tilted her chin and lowered his mouth to hers, and as their lips touched he felt her soften and rise to meet him. She wanted him too, and the relief of it filled him with joy. Gently, he pulled her closer, felt her body warm against his, her lips opening as he deepened his kiss.

He hadn't meant for it to happen, but now she was in his arms and everything was spinning out of control. He'd never kissed a more beautiful mouth, touched a milkier skin. He pulled the clip from her hair and tangled his hands in the endless beautiful softness of it.

How could he resist the pressure of her fingers at his neck, drawing him closer, the sensation of her body yielding to his? He'd let her in, allowed himself a taste of what that invisible, immutable force had been driving him towards for days, and he knew that he could lose himself at any moment.

He pulled away breathlessly. He could walk away now and there'd be no harm done, but her eyes held his and they were hazy with desire. Suddenly he was lifting her into his arms, carrying her to the hammock, laying her down.

She gasped softly against his neck as he hitched her leg up and drew her body firmly against him. And then his mouth was on hers again and it felt to Cormac that they might have fused into a single entity, driven by physical yearning and some other inexpressible emotion. Desperate to touch her, he pulled the cardigan away from her shoulders—then froze.

What was he doing? He had no right to be happy—he didn't deserve this beautiful girl.

'What's wrong?' Her voice was breathless, husky with desire.

He twisted away, then levered himself off the hammock with a strangled sigh. 'I can't do this.'

She struggled up and looked at him in confusion. 'What are you talking about?'

He shook his head and stepped back. 'It's a mistake. I shouldn't have stayed.'

She scrambled off the hammock and took a cautious step towards him. 'Did I do something wrong?'

He waltzed backwards, riding the wave of pain coursing through him. 'No, you didn't; it's not you, Milla—it's me. I'm not in a good place.'

He turned to walk away and felt her hand on his arm.

'If you're not in a good place, then go somewhere better. You don't have to live under that cloud.'

Her words jumbled chaotically in his head. He couldn't cope with words right now. Gently, he lifted her hand from his arm. 'I'm sorry.'

He turned and strode quickly towards the car.

'A kiss like that could never be a mistake, Cormac!'

Her words rang out behind him and momentarily stopped him in his tracks, then he wrenched open the door, started the engine and accelerated up the rise before he could change his mind.

CHAPTER SEVEN

MILLA SLID DOWN onto the decking with her mug in her hands. She'd hit another wall with her work and this time it was Cormac's fault. How could she concentrate on anything after last night? How she'd craved the solitude of the bothy, but there was no peace here now. Only confusion and pain.

Why had she even asked him to stay and watch the lights with her? She had no answer, except that she'd enjoyed his company in the restaurant and then he'd become withdrawn. She'd seen that familiar pain in his eyes and she'd wanted to know more about him.

But she hadn't intended to unravel him like a spool of thread.

When his eyes locked on hers it made her head spin. She'd wondered sometimes if he was drawn to her in some way too, but he'd taken her by surprise with his kiss, then surprised her again by backing off.

She sipped her coffee without tasting it. The way his mouth had felt on hers…the way he'd buried his hands in her hair… She could still feel the deep warmth of him, but she was a fool.

It's not you. It's me.

It was the oldest line in the book. He'd kissed her, then decided he didn't want her. She put down her coffee. Another rejection… Perhaps she really *was* unlovable. And yet the way he'd looked at her, the way he'd pulled her against him… She'd thought she'd felt something real.

She wished she could talk to her mother. Colleen had understood people so well, seen things in them that Milla hadn't. She wondered what her mother would advise her to do—and then she remembered how Colleen had said that you could only ever follow the road you were on in the best way you could.

It was how she'd accepted her illness, why she'd worn her bright scarves and carried on doing the things she loved until she hadn't been able to do them any more.

Milla swiped at her cheeks with her hands and got to her feet. She would push through somehow. Prioritise work and forget everything else. Her ankle was improving—she was barely limping today. Perhaps she'd take her sketchbook and go out. Losing herself in the landscape would heal her spirit.

She was on her way inside when she heard the rumble of an engine. With a thumping heart she watched as a familiar vehicle appeared over the rise and descended towards the bothy. As it drew nearer she squinted at the windscreen, feeling both relief and disappointment when she saw Sam at the wheel.

He parked, jumped from the cab and hurried towards her. 'Hi, Milla. How's your foot?'

Sam was so easy to be around. She smiled. 'Much better, thanks. I'm hardly limping today.'

'That's good.' A sudden seriousness broke in his features. 'I'm sorry to disturb you, but we've had a phone call at the house. Someone called Daniel Calder-Jones wants to speak to you—he says it's urgent.'

She felt the colour draining from her face. 'Daniel?'

Sam nodded. 'Yes. I told him I'd come and fetch you. He wants you to call him straight back.'

She didn't want to speak to Dan—urgent or not—but then she felt her heart stall. Had something happened at home? She dismissed the thought instantly. Her father would have called, or one of her brothers—they had the number for Calcarron House after all. No, Dan was calling about something else.

She felt a prickle of irritation. He'd probably

lost the password for his online banking—in Dan's world that would qualify as an emergency. But, whatever it was, if she went with Sam at least she'd be able to retrieve her own vehicle, which was still at the house. She only hoped she wouldn't bump into Cormac.

She looked at Sam and frowned. 'Okay…well, I suppose I'd better come with you.'

Cormac crouched down to check the connecting lugs on the last length of aluminium edging, then rose to his feet. The marquee company had done a good job, but his army training compelled him to check everything. He surveyed the gleaming parquet, scanning the surface for any gaps that might catch an unsuspecting stiletto heel, but it was perfect. Now he could move on to the exterior lighting. He needed to focus on his tasks and keep his thoughts tightly leashed. It was the only way he would get through the day.

Last night he'd lain awake for hours, then slept fitfully, his desert nightmares spiked with emerald skies and the taste of whiskey in her mouth. He should never have kissed her; he should never have allowed himself even to think of caring for her, but the worst of it was that she'd wanted him too.

He'd suddenly realised that he couldn't let

ELLA HAYES   153

that happen—couldn't let her develop feelings for him. He had nothing to give—and besides, he had every intention of going on tour again, and if was killed, like Duncan, then she'd be left alone, like Emma. He couldn't do that to her. She'd already been through enough with Daniel.

The electrician was making his way across the lawn with a toolbox and nodded affably in Cormac's direction as he passed. 'We've got a nice dry day. If it holds, we'll be rigged by late afternoon.'

Cormac nodded. 'Great! I'm going to check the generator...'

His words trailed away at the sound of a fast-approaching vehicle and he watched as the Jeep barrelled into view and screeched to a halt at the main door. He was about to shout a reprimand when he realised that Sam was hurrying to the passenger side to open the door for someone, and when Milla eased herself down from the cab his heart stood still.

As if she could sense him she looked up, held his gaze, then turned away and followed Sam into the house.

Cormac's heart was racing. What was she doing here? And why had she disappeared into the house in such a hurry?

As she'd gazed at him across the lawn he'd noticed the shadows under her eyes, the pallor of her skin. All his fault. He'd hurt her, and he couldn't stand it.

He ran his hands through his hair and turned away from the house. He thought he'd patched up his armour and hardened his heart, but seeing her like this had thrown him into turmoil.

He closed his eyes, forced his breathing into a slower rhythm and started towards the generator shed. Then he stopped, turned, and strode back towards the house.

Milla stared at the number scrawled on the notepad. Whatever was going on, Dan was evidently still in Berlin. She glanced at the door. Sam had reassured her that she wouldn't be disturbed, but she felt skittish. Seeing Cormac like that…and now calling Dan, not knowing what she was going to hear…

She took a deep breath and tapped out the number.

When he answered, his voice was low and smoky. 'Milla, baby—why on earth have you buried yourself in the back of beyond? It's taken me ages to track you down.'

He sounded all right—not injured or impaired. 'What's so urgent, Dan?'

'Straight to the point, as always.'

She imagined him raking long fingers through his hair.

'The truth is… I've been thinking things over and I realise I miss you. I miss you a lot.'

She hadn't known what to expect, but it wasn't this. 'You *miss* me?'

'I'm all over the place, Mills, and I can't stop thinking about your beautiful face, the way you anchor me. My little rock…remember?'

She couldn't believe what she was hearing. 'What I remember is you throwing your "little rock" into the lake and letting it sink.'

'I understand that you're angry, but I'll make it up to you.'

It was hard to keep her tone level. 'What happened to Maria?'

There was a long silence. 'She left.'

'Ah! I suppose that happened when you told her how much you were missing me…?'

'Don't be like that.'

'Like what? I'm just trying to get the facts straight, that's all.'

'Baby, please. I'm sorry. I made a massive mistake but I want to see you. I'll come to Scotland—this weekend!'

She pictured his face. Blue eyes, dark lashes, the aquiline nose with its silver ring. She remembered the fizz of pure joy she'd felt when he proposed, the ring glittering on her finger, but suddenly she couldn't remember why it had meant so much. Cormac's face slipped into her thoughts. Her broken soldier. If he hadn't bolted last night would she have rushed to call Dan back at all?

'Please, Milla. Give me another chance.'

She was shaking her head slowly, even though she knew he couldn't see. 'There'd be no point.'

'Why?'

'There'd be no point because I don't love you any more.'

'You're saying it's too late?' Even the tremor in his voice left her unaffected.

'It is. Goodbye, Dan.'

Softly, she put down the receiver.

She leaned over the desk and cradled her head in her hands. She had no regrets about turning him down—quite the opposite. She had closure.

The sound of a footstep at the door startled her and she looked up sharply as Cormac came in. He froze, and for an endless moment their eyes locked. He was unshaven, tired around the eyes. She thought she heard him catch his breath.

'I'm sorry—I didn't know you were—'

Her heart was hammering against her ribcage and she prayed her voice wouldn't tremble when she spoke. 'Don't worry. I was just leaving.'

She rose to her feet and took a step towards the door, but he was in the way and for some reason he wasn't moving.

His eyes clouded. 'I— Is everything okay…?'

She lifted her chin, tried to keep her tone cool and measured. 'Everything is perfect, thank you—except you're blocking the door.'

He opened his mouth as if he was about to say something, then closed it and stood back. As she walked past she caught the warm smell of him and it stirred the memory of his kiss, the delicious heat of his body crushed against hers. She felt light-headed. More than anything she wanted to turn around and demand an explanation, but instead she kept on walking and didn't look back.

On a different day she would have noticed the play of dappled light under the trees that covered the track to Strathburn. She would have admired the lime-green stands of young ferns and the clusters of spikey sedge, but not today. Today a storm was gathering in her mind and Cormac was at its eye.

Before she'd gone to the house she'd resolved to put last night behind her, but seeing him, feeling the heat of him so close, had stirred up all that emotion again. He'd barely said a word, just dangled in the awkward silence with his unfathomable gaze.

Who was Cormac Buchanan, anyway? Just

another incomprehensible male riding rough-shod over her emotions?

She felt bruised. Blue and purple and red were the colours which exploded in her head as pain throbbed inside her, and on top a layer of festering, furious anger which felt like yellow or ochre.

At the bothy, she slammed out of the car and marched into the studio. She rammed her iPod onto the dock, setting the volume to max, then mixed the colours she could see in her head and set to work, recreating the landscape she'd sketched the day before.

She knew the shapes and shadows of those rocks and she worked into them the livid colours of her pain. At times she discarded her brushes and used her fingers to drag furious seams of colour across the canvas. She didn't notice the time passing, or that she was thirsty. She didn't notice her paint-spattered clothes. She was lost in her creation and she had no care for ever being found.

Cormac leaned against the wall and closed his eyes. He should have said something, but the right words wouldn't come, and then she'd asked him to move away from the door and he'd had to let her go.

Her scent lingered in the air, dazing him, so

that he couldn't immediately remember why he'd come into the office—something to do with the hired generator.

He crossed to the desk and sank into the chair. He needed to concentrate. It was the hire agreement—there was something he wanted to check.

He reached for a stack of papers on the desk, then noticed the pad by the telephone. He picked it up. *Daniel Calder-Jones* and a number. Her ex-fiancé!

He had no claim on Milla, especially after last night, but that name drove a knife into his heart. She'd said it was over with Daniel, so why was she calling him?

He looked the note again, saw that it was Sam's writing. Sam would know what was going on.

He found his brother in the marquee, frowning at the contents of a small box. 'I think this order is wrong—Rosie's going to have a fit.'

'Is there a delivery note? I'll call to sort out a replacement if it's not right, so don't panic.'

Sam grinned. 'It's not me who'll be panicking.' He squinted at the box. 'I don't even know what organza bags are.'

'They're gift bags—for favours.' In spite of his dark mood, Sam's quizzical gaze made him smile. He shrugged. 'I had to fill over a hundred of them with whisky liqueurs on the morning of Duncan's wedding—someone had forgotten to do it.'

He ran a hand along a horizontal support, pretending to check it for stability.

'So, what was going on with Milla this morning?'

Sam lifted his eyebrows in a question.

'You raced up to the house like you were on fire.'

'Ah, that!' He grinned. 'I don't know much. This guy Daniel—her ex-fiancé, apparently— called this morning and said he needed to speak to her urgently. I told him she was at the bothy and he asked me if I could fetch her. So I did.'

'And?'

Sam had unearthed an invoice from inside the box and was scrutinising it. 'And I left her in the office, so she could call him back, and that was it. I didn't see her after that. She took her own car when she left.' He looked up, a glimmer of curiosity in his eyes. 'Why are you so interested in Milla all of a sudden?'

'I'm not interested in Milla—you caught my attention with your rally driver impression, that's all.' He motioned to the box in Sam's hand. 'Why don't you give me that and I'll go and check that they've sent us the right stuff?'

* * *

Cormac watched the electrician and his apprentice balancing on ladders, working their way across the marquee ceiling with a mesh of LED lights. It would be stunning when it was all done, but the rigging was laborious. He'd helped at first, but they were in a rhythm now, which meant he could escape for a while.

He ducked out of the marquee and followed a narrow path to the loch shore. At the water's edge he crouched to pick up a handful of flat stones and skimmed them deftly across the dark shifting water. He counted the jumps and thought of Duncan, of long-ago summer days when they'd competed for the most bounces or the furthest throwing distance. They'd been friends for ever, and shared so much, but those days were gone now.

He turned to look at the hills. He couldn't see the bothy from here, but knowing that Milla was there set his pulse racing. He shuddered as he recalled the cold light in her eyes, masking the hurt he knew she must be feeling. If only she knew that hurting her had been the last thing on his mind. Why had the right words eluded him?

He kicked a stone into the water. *Daniel Calder-Jones.* The very thought of the ex-fiancé turned him inside out and he didn't even understand why. He'd only known Milla for a matter of days, but she was making him feel things he didn't want to feel—couldn't allow himself to feel.

He dropped to his haunches and trawled the beach for more flat stones. Would she listen if he tried to explain?

At the sound of his name being called he rose to his feet. He was needed, and for a moment he was thankful—working stopped him thinking. Anything was better than thinking.

A shock of silence filled the studio as the music stopped. Milla half stumbled backwards and gazed at the immense canvas glistening on the easel in front of her. She didn't know what to make of it but somehow it didn't matter. She let the brush slip from her fingers and fall to the floor.

In the kitchen, she filled a glass with water and drank, then filled the glass again. The clock on the wall told her it was after four and she could barely believe it; the day had passed in a blur.

She wandered outside and sat on the edge of the hammock. Had the mystical energy of Northern Lights triggered this out-of-body experience? She looked at her paint-caked fingers, her black-encrusted fingernails. Her jeans and tee shirt were no better. She rolled the glass slowly across her forehead, felt its cold, hard kiss on her skin.

No. It wasn't the Aurora that had sent her spiralling into a dark rapture—she knew all too well what had fuelled the torrent of emotion she'd poured into her painting.

She looked across the hills and breathed in the sweet scent of the gorse. She'd promised herself a walk. It wasn't too late. She'd clean up and go out. Her ears were ringing from the rock music she'd been playing and now she craved the wild peace of the great outdoors. She wanted to lose herself in a larger canvas, take time to rest and fall back into her own head.

The late afternoon was golden. Spider webs glistened against the purples and greens of the heathland and tiny moths with pearly wings flitted from the heather as she brushed past. It was peaceful. The steady clomp of her walking boots and the random calls of a lapwing were the only sounds disturbing the vast hum of emptiness.

At the foot of the path that Cormac had pointed out to her she paused, considering her ankle, then started to climb. When she crested the ridge and levered herself through the gap in the rocks she knew it had been worth the risk.

The light at this time of day drew texture from every craggy surface, from every blade of waving golden grass. Below, Loch Calcarron stretched through the valley like a dark blue ribbon, impenetrable and mysterious. She crossed the terrace of stones carefully, testing each foothold, until she found a broad flat boulder with a stone backrest.

Cormac's favourite landscape stretched before her, wide and indifferent.

He'd been bemused at her fascination for the stones, but stones were like people in some ways. Touched by time, weathered by life. A smooth pebble could hide a diamond or be scarred with the dark fissures of emptiness. Cormac was a smooth pebble.

She pulled a sketchbook out of her bag and looked across the unfolding mountains and endless sky. She drew an idle line.

What was he hiding? She'd told herself she didn't care, but she was lying to herself. There was something about him, an ache of sadness behind his eyes, which spoke to her heart, made her want to understand.

She shaped an arc with her pencil, shaded it softly.

He'd hurt her last night, and infuriated her this morning, but now, sitting here in his special place, she knew he hadn't meant any of it.

She worked her pencil over the paper more quickly.

He'd taken her for dinner, kissed her in a way that had turned her inside out and then he'd abandoned her without explanation. Just thinking about it was stirring her up again because she couldn't rationalise it.

She wasn't good at uncertainty. She was a girl who circled landmarks on a road map so she knew she was travelling in the right direction. She sketched outlines before committing paint to canvas. She read instructions. She paid attention.

Until yesterday Cormac had kept his distance, yet her heart had dared to imagine a connection between them. Foolish heart.

She threw down her sketchbook and closed her eyes. The low sunshine spangled against her eyelids, the tiny explosions of red and silver filling her head. A pheasant squawked from somewhere down the hill, drummed its frantic wings in clumsy flight, and far, far away in the distance an engine throbbed faintly.

CHAPTER EIGHT

CORMAC SECURED THE last string of bulbs to a hook embedded in a tree limb and jumped down from the ladder. He'd spent the whole afternoon weaving lights through the trees to create the ultimate romantic backdrop for Rosie's evening wedding reception. It had been a painstaking process, but to his dismay, the work had not absorbed him.

With every wire he'd untangled and laid straight his insides had twisted into tighter knots and the hollow ache in his heart had grown stronger. How was it possible that he was missing someone he barely knew? Missing her sweet smile and mischievous eyes, missing the way her brow wrinkled when she frowned, missing her scent and the soft sound of her sigh.

'A kiss like that could never be a mistake, Cormac.'

Her words had stopped him in his tracks because he'd felt it too—the undeniable chemistry between them. It had taken a massive effort of will for him to drive away, but staying had not been an option. At least that was what he'd thought last night. But now he was in torment.

In the office, her eyes had flayed him where he'd stood, rendered him helpless. Stupidly dumb. He knew she'd been hiding behind that hard shell. It was her best defence and he understood that better than anyone—because he did the same thing all the time.

He looked across the lawn to the marquee. There was a radio playing, a tune rising above the sound of creaking ladders as the electricians finished the interior lighting. They didn't need him; it would be the perfect time to slip away quietly.

He didn't know exactly what he'd say to her, but suddenly the only thing he wanted to do was see her.

The sinking sun warmed his back as he hammered the quad bike up the slope. He remembered bringing her the bothy key that first afternoon. She'd been standing on the rise, a graceful silhouette, watching his approach with interest. She'd waved, but he hadn't waved back. He'd been nervous, wary of the casual temerity she'd displayed at the roadside, afraid that with a single kick of her boot she would turn him over like a pebble on the beach.

He looked upwards now, but the vantage point was deserted.

At the bothy he got off the quad and strode over the deck. A cloak of stillness hung around the building and for a moment he hesitated, before tapping on the door. He glanced across the track. Her vehicle was parked in its spot, so she must be here. He knocked again, more loudly but still there was no sound from inside. He tried the door. It was unlocked.

'Milla?'

He stepped inside and called again.

'Milla!'

Perhaps she was too absorbed to hear him. Cautiously, he walked to the studio door and pushed it open.

For a moment he stared at the huge painting in shock—it was a staggering landscape, but it was no pastoral idyll. Yesterday she'd told him that her final artwork would be done in oils, but he'd had no idea how complete a transformation it would be.

The work in front of him was like a battle scene, ominous and strangely visceral. Perhaps it was because of the paint, still wet in patches, its thick seams of red and gold glistening like open wounds.

He tore his eyes away and looked around the silent studio. The palette she'd been using was parked on the bench whilst a paintbrush, clotted with colour, lay abandoned on the floor.

He stepped outside and onto the deck in a kind of daze. Milla's painting had affected him deeply. It was raw and angry—a vivid reminder of the pain he tried to bury but couldn't. He paced the boards, tormented by a confusion of images he couldn't bear to see, until the piercing cry of a bird brought him back into the moment.

He sat down on the edge of the hammock and lifted his face to the breeze. A hare lolloped across the track, then paused, regarding him with its steady, amber eye. As he gazed at it he remembered watching Milla walk into the house that morning; walking without a limp. If her foot was better and she'd gone for a walk he knew exactly where she'd be.

He rose to his feet, strode to the quad and started the engine.

He stepped through the gap in the rocks and looked along the ridge. She was there, exactly where he'd thought she'd be, leaning against a boulder, her sketchbook by her side. She was wearing combat pants and a tee shirt, but she didn't look tough. She looked sweet and slightly vulnerable.

'Milla!'

The sound of her name blew back at him on the breeze and disappeared over the heather. She didn't move. Her eyes were closed—maybe she was sleeping.

He made his way across the rocks towards her and called again, softly. 'Milla…'

With a startled jerk she turned in his direction and scrambled to her feet. The breeze lifted loose strands of hair around her face and she pushed them away, then fixed him with a cool green gaze.

'I'm sorry if I frightened you… I thought I'd find you here.'

She pushed her hands into her pockets. 'So you're a detective now? What do you want, Cormac?'

He'd expected this. The cool edge in her voice, the defensive glint in her eye.

'I—I want to say sorry about last night.' He moistened his lips hesitantly. 'I want you to give me a chance to explain—'

She turned away. 'There's no need. You kissed me—you changed your mind. There's nothing to explain. I'd like you to go now.'

He gritted his teeth; this was all his fault and he had to put it right. He laid a gentle hand on her arm. Her skin was pale and smooth beneath his fingers.

'Milla, look at me, please.'

Slowly she turned and lifted glistening eyes to his.

'Don't cry.' He chased her tears away with a thumb. 'You're so wrong. I didn't kiss you and change my mind. I kissed you and nearly lost my mind...'

'I don't understand—'

The confusion and sweet hope he could see in her gaze was too much for him, and before he could stop himself he was pulling her into his arms. It felt so completely right that he almost couldn't breathe. He wanted to lift her face and kiss her as he'd kissed her before, but that would be a mistake. A mistake he couldn't make again.

Reluctantly he released her and stepped back. 'We need to talk, and then you'll understand.' He motioned for them to sit down, then he drew in a steadying breath.

'A year ago, I lost my best friend...'

As his words fell into the space between them he could hardly believe that the relentless pulse of his pain could already be a year old. She said nothing, but he felt her hand sliding over his.

He lifted unseeing eyes to the view. *"A British soldier has been killed in Afghanistan while serving with the Royal Engineers. The Ministry of Defence has said the serviceman was killed in action by enemy fire on an operation to the*

*east of Kabul on Monday. He has not yet been
named but his family have been informed."'*

He felt the bile rising in his throat.

'That was the newspaper coverage. Fifty
words. Duncan gave his life and they gave him
fifty words in a newspaper.'

A wave of nausea gripped him and he rocked
forward, drawing his hands over his head.
Fighting this bitter grief was a war he usually
waged in private. Somehow Milla's presence
was sharpening the agony, threatening to derail
him completely. He'd thought he could talk to
her, but now he was unsure.

He was about to rise to his feet and leave
when he felt her arm sliding around him, her
hand moving over his back and shoulders.

He shuddered and lifted his head. 'We were
assembling an assault bridge outside Kabul—
training a handful of infantry guys. With a fully
trained troop building a bridge takes minutes,
but for some reason it was dragging on. The
light was fading, and at the far end of the bridge
there was a problem. We weren't in an active
combat area, but there was something in the
air… I had a bad feeling… I didn't want to send
any of the sappers across. I was going to go myself, but then a call came through from base and
I had to take it. I saw Duncan heading over the

bridge and I couldn't stop him, because I had an officer bending my ear.'

He could still taste the dust in his mouth, hear the sickening whine of enemy fire tearing through the darkening desert.

'There was no warning. They just tore into us. It wasn't a battle; it was an assassination. There were fifteen of us out there, but Duncan was the only man on the bridge—he was an easy target. The force of the shot knocked him right over the rail.'

Cormac pressed his palms to his eyes and felt Milla's arm tightening around him.

'Everyone hit the ground and stayed down. We were wearing flak vests and helmets, but I'd seen… I crawled out to where he was, but before I reached him I knew…'

He could feel the shuddering sobs building now and bit them back hard.

'He'd been hit in the neck. There was so much…' He dropped his head into his hands, his tongue thick with words. 'So much blood. He didn't look like a man any more. He looked like a red stain in the sand.'

Words wouldn't come now. Only those bleak images unspooling in his head like a nightmare. The sliding zip on the body bag, Emma's face bleached as white as the lilies on the coffin. Little Jamie…

Cormac forced himself to breathe, forced himself to focus on the sensation of Milla's hand stroking his shoulder. 'It should have been me. It was down to me and he went instead. He had a wife, a baby. All those lives destroyed because I was on the phone.'

Both her arms were around him now, holding him as he battled the onslaught of emotion. The sun's rays weakened and the bird calls dwindled. They sat for a long time until he felt calm enough to speak again.

'I'd known Duncan all my life. We were at school together. Joined up together...did our training together. He was like a brother.' He shook his head and sighed. 'I can't begin to explain the size of the hole he's left in my life. Every smile feels like a betrayal, so I don't smile. Duncan will never smile or laugh again, so how can I? Every single day is hard because nothing makes sense to me any more.'

There was a gleam of tears in her eyes and he couldn't bear the weight of her empathy.

He gazed into the distance. 'My father wants me to leave the army and take over the estate, but I can't. It would be like giving up on Duncan and on everything we stood for. I love it here, but I'm not ready to bury myself at Calcarron. I trained to do a job and I want to go back and do it. If I was spared that day, then I need to believe there's a reason—that there's something I've still got to do. But they won't let me go overseas. They think I'll become unhinged and do something reckless.'

Milla thought about the photograph she'd seen in Angus's studio. Two friends with wide, happy smiles. Duncan's death had tested Cormac to the limit, but he had innate strength—not only physical strength, but an immense strength of character too. She'd known that about him right away. He'd make it through—he just needed time, that was all, and she understood that better than anybody.

'I'm sorry for everything that's happened to you. Words are never enough.'

There was a raw ache in his eyes as he turned to look at her, and she knew that he needed something from her that went beyond a simple expression of condolence.

She drew her legs up and hugged her knees. 'My mother died when I was fifteen and it still hurts.' She felt a lump rising in her throat and swallowed hard. 'It wasn't dramatic, like your friend's death, but watching someone you love die slowly is… Well, I suppose it's torture of a different kind. I'm ashamed to admit that I felt she'd betrayed me by dying. I felt her love for me should have been strong enough to keep her alive. It was childish, I know, but by dying, she made me feel unlovable.'

His eyes clouded. 'I'm sorry. Losing your mother so young...' His words trailed away, overtaken by a quickening breeze.

'Young or old, it's like you said the other night. Pain is pain whenever it comes.' She shivered a little. 'You didn't have to tell me about Duncan.'

He wiped his face with his hands. 'I did—because of what happened last night.'

'I don't understand...'

He let out a short, bitter laugh. 'I'm a total screw-up, Milla. Can't you see that? I don't sleep; I'm on a short fuse all the time. I don't know why I'm alive or what I'm supposed to do with myself. I can't be normal. Last night... Maybe it was the Northern Lights or maybe it was the whiskey. Or maybe it was because of you...'

His eyes lingered on hers and she felt a familiar tug of longing.

'I never meant to kiss you, but somehow it happened and it shook me up. *You* really shook me up and I didn't know what to do. I'm not used to...' He fell silent.

'Not used to what? Letting go? Letting yourself feel something that doesn't hurt?'

He nodded slowly. 'Something like that.'

He plucked a stem of grass from a crevice and broke it between his fingers. 'When I saw you this morning I couldn't find the right words. I could see how much I'd hurt you and I never meant to do that. Last night I left because of me, not because of you, and it was incredibly hard to walk away because you were right.'

'About what?'

His eyes filled with soft light. 'About that kiss.'

She couldn't stop her lips curling into a smile. 'So what do we do about it?'

To her amazement, the light drained from his eyes and he stood up.

'We're not going to do anything about it. That's why I came to find you—I didn't want you to think that you'd done something wrong, or that I didn't feel it too, but there's no future in it.'

Why did she feel as if the earth was tilting on its axis? 'No future?'

He searched her face with pleading eyes. 'I'm not what you need, Milla. I don't want you to care about me because I'll only let you down—like I let Duncan down.' He faltered. 'Besides, there's Daniel…'

She scrambled to her feet. 'Daniel! What's he got to do with anything?'

Cormac's eyes narrowed. 'You called him… I thought—'

'I called him *back*! He sent Sam to fetch me on some pretext of urgency, but it wasn't urgent. His lover has left him and he's got a notion into his head that he wants us to try again. He didn't factor in the possibility that I might not love him any more.'

Cormac's eyes softened fleetingly. 'He was an idiot to let you go in the first place, but I'm no better. I've hurt you as well, and I don't want to do it again.'

He was pulling down the shutters and she couldn't let it happen. She was about to protest when a crack of thunder split the air and the heavens opened.

Numb with shock, she looked up and around. A vast dark cloud had sailed across the sky behind them, polarising the last of the sunlight into a sliver of sharp contrast which sliced through the landscape like a silver blade. Darkness and light…suspended in a moment of sublime harmony.

The scene seemed to mirror her situation with Cormac—shared moments of beauty and blinding light threatened by storm clouds.

Fat drops of rain splattered down and spread across her tee shirt, but she didn't move. The kiss of cool rain on her face drowned the swell of hopeless tears she didn't want him to see.

She didn't understand why she was crying; she didn't understand why her heart was aching.

Within moments the rain was lashing down in vertical columns, splashing on stones, sucking and gurgling though the rocks. She felt water trickling down her back and shivered. Beside her Cormac stood, his bare arms glistening, hair darkly plastered to his head.

He opened his palms to the downpour. 'Typical May weather—four seasons in one day. Have you got a jacket?'

He seemed to have reverted to his old persona. Polite, detached. How could he switch channels so easily?

She raised her voice over the drumming of the rain. 'I didn't think I'd need it.' She looked down at her sodden clothes. 'It's too late now, anyway.'

He raked the water out of his hair. 'We should go. The stones are slippery, so watch your step.' He paused for a moment, then held out his hand. 'Here. Take my hand. We don't want a repeat performance with that ankle.'

His gaze was neutral, but deliberately so, and she realised that he was battling with himself after all. She slipped her fingers into his, felt the shock of warmth as their palms kissed.

He led her carefully across the rocks, the wet cling of his tee shirt moulding to his body, narrow rivulets of water sliding down his cheeks as he turned to check her progress. He went ahead through the gap in the rocks, then reached for her hand once more. The steep path was running with water, loose grit shining and sliding beneath their feet, but Cormac moved with a surefooted animal grace.

His grip on her hand was firm as he navigated the downward slope, and when he turned to look back at her she couldn't stop her eyes drifting to his mouth. That kiss. She couldn't shake the memory of it, and she knew he was feeling it too.

At the foot of the slope he let go and swiped the moisture off his face. 'The quad's not built for two, but we'll manage somehow—unless you'd rather walk in the rain?'

She shook her head, not daring to speak.

His eyes travelled over her face and wet clothes. 'Come on—you're shivering. Let's get you back to the bothy.'

He walked to the quad, reached for the ignition—then stopped. She watched the faltering heave of his chest, the slow shift of his shoulders, and then he was turning around, striding back towards her. He paused for a moment, his eyes burning with all the light he'd been trying to hide, then he took her face into his hands and pressed his forehead to hers.

'I can't do it. I can't keep you at arm's length, Milla. Forgive me.'

And then his lips were on hers, cool rain mingling with the heat of his kiss. He pulled her closer until she was lost in the sensation of wet skin, wet clothes and his perfect mouth.

Everything about this felt right—the scent of soap and rain, the intoxicating warmth of his body pressed against hers. And as they kissed under darkening skies a steady pulse of calm flooded her veins as if her atoms had realigned themselves with his and exhaled a thankful sigh.

Yet again he'd broken the promises he'd made to himself—but what else could he have done? It had been impossible not to kiss her...the way she'd been looking at him, with the rain coming down, her skin dripping. But it had been more than that.

Maybe it had been because of the way she'd held him, the way she'd listened, the way she'd shared her own grief. Or maybe it had been there from the beginning, when he'd stopped to help her on the road. From the moment she'd looked into his eyes he'd felt something shifting inside his heart—like a tiny crack of light appearing in the dark. He'd tried so hard to stop its trickling glow, but now, as he drove them through the downpour, he recognised that light for what it was.

He knew he was out of whack, but Milla lightened him, made him feel young again. She was smart and funny and she spoke her mind. She didn't tiptoe around him like other people did. But he was scared. Scared of letting her into his heart because that meant letting Duncan go. Moving on with life, falling in love, laughing, smiling—all those things Duncan had lost.

Could there be a way through the guilt? A way of living that didn't feel like betrayal?

He had to try. She made him want to try. He liked the feel of her arms around him, the crush of her softness at his back they hurtled through the heather and accelerated up the slope.

The warmth of her cheek bloomed against his shoulder and he wondered what she was thinking. He wondered if she wanted him as desperately as he wanted her.

The bothy was filled with the low, brooding light of the storm. It felt strange to be here, knowing what he wanted to do, and although they'd kissed passionately just minutes ago he felt a strange heaviness in his limbs, a confusion of emotions stirring his heart. Kissing her was easy, but when it came to seduction he was seriously out of practice. He'd have to take it slow—acclimatise.

He reached his fingers to the curve of her cheek, brushed her lower lip softly with his thumb. 'You're trembling.'

'I'm not trembling—I'm shivering.' She looked down at the water puddling at their feet, then smiled softly. 'Wait here. I'll get a towel.'

As she disappeared he wondered if she'd sensed his apprehension. Perhaps she was feeling it too.

He crossed to the wood burner and set a fire. He stared into the flames until they morphed into flickering abstracts. He thought about the phoenix. Could Milla raise him from his ashes?

He turned at the sound of her footsteps and reached for the towel in her hand, but she held it away, a mischievous gleam in her eye. He dropped his hands and she stepped closer. Gently, she blotted his face, his head and the back of his neck.

He felt the plush cotton sliding down his arms and over his hands, and then the hem of his tee shirt rising as she peeled it upwards over his torso. He pulled it over his head, heard the wet slap as it landed on the floor. She held his gaze as she pressed the towel to his chest, then worked it over his abdomen.

When he felt her fingers moving over his skin, her lips warm against his shoulder, he closed his eyes. This was living. Feeling the touch of another person…being touched by the person you loved.

He opened his eyes. 'Your turn.'

He'd been aroused from the moment she'd touched him, but it was nothing to how he felt now. He smoothed the towel down her arms, kissed her fingers softly, then slowly pulled her tee shirt over her head. Her skin was pale, peppered with tiny goosebumps, her nipples taut against the lacy fabric of her bra.

He moistened his lips. He wanted to touch her there, but instead he traced the curve of her waist with his fingers, felt the slip of moisture clinging to her skin. He picked up the towel again and dried her stomach, her shoulders and her back, caressing her with its softness until he could feel warmth radiating from her body.

Her hair was saturated. Carefully, he unfastened the clip and uncoiled its golden lengths into the towel, squeezing out the water until it fell around her face in a damp tumble. Then he lifted it aside so he could press his lips to the nape of her neck. She sank against him, skin to skin, and sighed softly. Dizzy with longing, he turned her around, tilted her chin and grazed her lips with his.

He slipped his fingers into the waistband of her trousers. 'We should take these off.'

She stepped back and held his gaze as she slid

them over her hips and down her legs. Her body
glowed in the firelight, shadows slipping into
dusky hollows. He wanted to visit those hollows
with his mouth, kiss every beautiful inch, but
something in his head was beginning to swirl.

She was stepping closer, running her hands
up his arms, over his shoulders to his face. She
pulled his mouth to hers and it was warm, soft
like ripe fruit, sweet and filled with yearning.
He wanted to dive in, but a wave was crashing
over him, threatening to knock him sideways.

She pulled away. 'What's wrong, Cor? Am
I losing you?'

The light was low, but he could hear the catch
in her voice, see the doubt in her eyes. He took
her face in his hands, traced the swell of her
lower lip with his thumb. He had to give himself permission to be happy again, and Milla
made him happy. He had to let her in, surren-
der to his desire.

He leaned in and kissed her softly. 'No, you're
not losing me. I was only thinking that now
would be a good time to take this upstairs.'

CHAPTER NINE

THE FIRST THING he noticed was the stab of sunshine slicing through the mezzanine. The second thing he noticed was the sound of Milla's gentle breathing. He turned over and lost himself in the view. She looked like an angel, with a golden tangle of hair spilling across the pillow and around her face. Momentarily her lips moved, as if in prayer, and he felt a strange wave of euphoria building in his chest. She sighed softly and reached a hand to his shoulder, then fell back into her dreams.

Her hand felt warm, and he remembered the way she'd touched him just hours ago, her slow kisses trailing down his abdomen. He felt a flicker of desire and closed his eyes. Was this happiness really his to own?

He moved a lock of hair away from her face and wondered if she'd soothed his spirit as well as his body and his heart. The nightmares hadn't come. For the first time in months he hadn't

woken up in a pool of Duncan's blood, screaming his fury into the darkening desert sky.

He rolled onto his back and stared at the ceiling. Was Emma managing to move on with her
life now? Was she coping?

He felt ashamed. If he'd been in touch more
often he'd know how she was, but lately he'd
kept his distance. He'd tried to be there for her,
but Duncan had died on his watch and he saw
it in her eyes every time she looked at him. He
was so tired of the guilt. It was always simmer-
ing, ready to break the surface and throw him
into turmoil. Seeing Emma's pain had simply
become unbearable.

He glanced at the bedside clock. No one
would ask him about his overnight absence, but
he would limit the damage if he could slip into
the house before anyone was awake.

As if she could sense his intention, Milla's
fingers flexed on his shoulder and she opened
sleepy eyes.

'Don't go.'

He shifted closer and pulled her into his arms.
'I don't want to, but I've got to get back.'

She pressed her lips to his neck. 'Will I see
you later?'

He buried his lips into her hair. 'Wild horses
wouldn't stop me.'

She pulled away and touched his mouth. 'This is new…'

He laughed. 'What?'

She traced the outline of his lips with her finger. 'This smile.' She eyed him mischievously. 'You should wear it more often. It suits you.'

'You're up early!' Rosie plonked herself down at the kitchen table and pulled her hair into an elastic band.

Cormac sighed. He'd been hoping for some time alone. He lifted a second mug off the dresser. 'So are you. Do you want coffee?'

She nodded, pulling and pushing at her hairstyle. 'I'm too wired to sleep. There seems to be so much to do and I keep thinking I've forgotten something.'

He shook his head. 'The only thing that really matters is that Fraser pitches up—preferably on time. Everything else is decoration.' He poured coffee into their mugs and added milk.

Rosie lifted an eyebrow. 'You'd better watch your step—telling a designer that "everything else is decoration" is like waving a red rag at a bull… By the way, you're humming.'

He felt a little ripple of shock. He hadn't noticed himself humming. 'Sorry.'

She sighed. 'I haven't heard you hum in a long time.'

He handed her a mug. 'I'm limbering up for the hymns. Consider it a wedding gift—the gift of not embarrassing your sister with bad singing on her wedding day: priceless.'

She sipped her coffee and eyed him quizzically. 'Ah—humour. Humming *and* humour. You remind me of a brother I had once…'

There was something unsettling about her expression. Was the change in him so obvious? He'd barely had time to get used to the idea of Milla himself, without being forensically examined by Rosie, but he could see the cogs in her brain turning and he grew wary.

'You haven't had dinner with us for two nights in a row…'

His unease intensified.

'You were wearing those clothes yesterday…'

She was scrutinising his face now, and he knew that she wasn't going to let it go.

'You haven't shaved this morning—'

'Rosie, would you just stop, please? I don't want—'

She put her mug down and pinned him with a wide blue stare. 'It's Milla, isn't it?'

Milla set down her brush and stood back. This new painting was as dramatic as the last one, but her motivating passion and inspiration came from a different place. It was an abstract work of jutting rocks in a stormy landscape, a brilliant sliver of light dissecting the inky clouds, trailing skeins of silver across the heavy sky. It represented her feelings for Cormac, and already she could feel its power.

She smiled to herself. She couldn't stop smiling this morning. Cormac had found a home in her heart and nothing had ever felt so perfect. A fizzing happiness tingled in her veins every time she thought of him.

She traced a finger over her lower lip, remembering the warmth of his mouth on her neck, the delicious shock of his skin against hers, the long, slow kisses that had turned her inside out. The way his body had fitted to hers, the way he'd taken his time and loved her so completely, until she was aching from the sweetness of it. The way that she had seen forever in his eyes.

Afterwards, he'd wrapped her in his arms and they'd talked into the night.

She'd told him more about Colleen's influence on her decision to become an artist, about the galleries they'd visited together even when Colleen had been dying. She'd cried a little when she'd told him how much she still missed her, and she'd laughed a little remembering her father's efforts to step into her mother's shoes. His woeful attempts at plaiting her hair for school, how he'd tried to make her favourite apple dumplings the way her mother had.

Cormac had told her about the work he'd been doing all over the world: sinking boreholes to supply clean water for communities in Sierra Leone, stabilising buildings in war-torn cities, setting things to rights wherever and whenever he could. He'd said he still had nightmares about the attack in the desert, but he hadn't talked more about Duncan and she hadn't pushed him—he would tell her in his own time.

She shook herself back to the moment. She'd promised Cormac a picture of Calcarron for Rosie's wedding present and she intended to keep her word, but she'd need to look at the scene again, make notes for colours, maybe take some photos on her phone.

She felt her mouth quirking into little smile. And if she bumped into Cormac while she was there then so much the better—their lovemaking had intensified her feelings for him and she was missing him already.

This morning the village sparkled, washed clean by the storm. Lingering puddles reflected the cobalt sky while petunias glistened in saturated hanging baskets. A man was sweeping the pavement outside the hotel. A postman clicked through a gate with a bag hanging off his shoulder.

As she drove along the main street these small scenes of village life warmed Milla's soul. On these streets there was a sense of quiet indifference to the outside world. Perhaps it was simple geography—London stood in awe of its own landmarks, but here everything was humbled by the landscape.

Today she felt no trepidation as she drove through the gates to Calcarron House. She was happy to be there. And as the big house came into view she was struck with how resplendent it looked in the slanting sunshine. Two new planters had been installed on either side of the grand entrance: twin box trees clipped into tidy spirals, their precision carelessly ignored by the scrambling clematis which flexed its milky petals against the mellow stone.

She parked and jumped down from the driver's seat. Looking across the lawn to the huge marquee, it dawned on her just how magnificent Rosie's wedding was going to be. Blinded by her own antipathy, she hadn't paid attention before, but now she could see the true scale of the wedding being organised here, could feel the buzz of excitement in the air, and to her astonishment she realised that her negative feelings had disappeared.

She was even contemplating a closer in-
spection of the marquee when a pair of hands
covered her eyes. She squealed in fright, then
laughed as Cormac spun her round.

'This is a nice surprise! What are you doing
here?'

His smile was the smile from the photograph,
and as she looked at him she felt a surge of happiness. 'I promised you a painting for Rosie, so
I thought I'd better get on with it—there's not
much time.'

His eyes filled with concern. 'But what about
your own work? I wasn't going to hold you to
a pledge made under desperate circumstances.'

The way he was looking at her made her wish
that they weren't standing in plain view of the
house. 'I knew you'd say that, but I want to do
it, Cor—for you.'

He glanced at the marquee. 'I could spare
half an hour—do you want me to carry your
sketchbook?'

She felt her lips curving into a smile. 'That
would be great—because, as you know, it's
rather heavy.'

He leaned into the vehicle, pulled out her bag
and threw it over his shoulder. 'Okay, then, let's
get out of here.'

They walked towards the loch, then took the
path that wound its way through the trees. When

they were hidden from view he dropped the bag and pulled her into his arms.

'You wouldn't believe how much I've missed you.'

He traced the line of her jaw with his thumb and then his mouth was on hers, warm and urgent. He kissed her until her insides were churning, then released her breathlessly.

She slipped her hands to his face, drank in the light in his eyes. 'I would, because I've missed you too.'

He sighed and pressed his forehead to hers. 'I should warn you—Rosie guessed where I was last night.'

Her stomach knotted. She hadn't given a thought to his family or how they might react. She suddenly wished she hadn't told Sam that she'd been engaged—she hadn't told Sam the whole story and a broken engagement could make her seem flaky.

'And—?'

He released her and stepped back, his eyes serious. 'You have to understand that my family see me as some kind of invalid. They want me to be healed, so they're grateful for any small miracles.'

'Is that what they think I am? It sounds like a lot to live up to.'

He pulled her into his arms and kissed her

hair. 'Don't worry. Rosie's under strict instructions not to make anything of it. I don't want us to be the centre of attention.'

She lifted her face to look at him. 'There's a big wedding going on—Rosie's going to be the centre of attention. No one's going to take any notice of us.'

'I hope you're right.' He picked up her bag and took her hand. 'Come on. I can't stay away too long. Deliveries are coming in thick and fast and I'm on inventory duty.'

Milla sat on the boulder she'd used before and pulled the sketchpad onto her knee. She had the bones of Rosie's painting in her head, but she needed to pin down colour and tone.

She was sketching outlines and making notes when she became aware of Cormac's gaze. She looked up. He was sitting a short distance away, throwing little stones into the water, but his eyes were trained on her.

She tried to ignore the tiny throb of longing she could feel in her veins. 'I can't work if you stare at me like that.'

'I can't help it.' He got to his feet and came to stand behind her. 'I want to see what you're doing.'

She tipped her head back to look at him. 'It's mostly outlines and notes about colour—it's not that interesting.'

He leaned over, grazed her forehead with his lips, then straddled the boulder behind her. His voice was a low murmur in her ear. 'I think it's very interesting.'

She felt his arms around her waist hugging her closer. She could feel the warmth of his chest against her back.

She feigned irritation. 'I won't be able to concentrate if you're sitting behind me.'

He ran his hands slowly down her arms and covered her hands with his. 'Show me how you draw. I see you doing that thing with the pencil where you hold it up and squint and I don't know what you're doing.'

The feel of his body was distracting, and she fought the urge to turn and pull his mouth to hers. 'All right. If I show you one thing will you let me get on with the rest?'

He brushed warm lips against her ear. 'Maybe…'

'Okay. We'll need a new page.'

She was turning the page when a sudden gust of wind whipped back several pages at once, revealing a half-finished pencil portrait.

He leaned across her shoulder and reached for the book. 'It's me…'

She stared at the drawing, as astonished as he was, and then she remembered. Yesterday, at the ridge, she'd been thinking about him, doodling with her pencil. She hadn't even been conscious of what she'd been drawing, just like that first time.

She tilted her head to one side, trying to decide if it was good or not. 'Don't let it go to your head...'

'You told me you don't like doing portraits.'

She twisted around to look at him, felt the heat of his slow-burn stare. 'That's right. I must have been very distracted.'

He lifted a hand to her face and brushed her lips with his. 'Are you distracted now?'

She felt her lips curving into a smile. 'Not yet, but I have a feeling that's about to change...'

At the edge of the treeline, Cormac pulled her into his arms for a last kiss. The thought of her going back to the bothy was suddenly unbearable. 'Will you come in for coffee before you go?'

'I shouldn't. I need to get this painting done—otherwise it'll still be wet when you give it to the happy couple.'

He buried his lips into her hair. 'They won't be opening any presents until they come back from honeymoon—you've got time for coffee. The bottom line is, I don't want you to go.'

He felt her face nuzzling into his neck. 'I don't want to go either, so I guess that's a yes to coffee.'

* * *

It was immediately obvious to Cormac that Rosie had told his mother. Lily was arranging flowers in a vase at the kitchen table and had carefully avoided meeting his eye when they'd come in. Instead, she was directing her full attention to Milla, asking about her ankle and how things were going with her painting.

He watched from the sidelines, preoccupied with his own thoughts. He knew he was falling for Milla, but he didn't feel ready to share it—it seemed pre-emptive. At the same time, he couldn't really blame Rosie for betraying his confidence. His family had been concerned about him ever since Duncan had died. Milla was the miracle they'd been waiting for—she was his proof of life.

'I'm getting into my stride now and I'm enjoying it,' Milla was saying. 'The studio at the bothy is wonderful—such a lovely space.'

He watched his mother poke a stout fern into the vase behind a bright orange daisy.

'Well, that's good to hear.' She looked up at Milla and smiled. 'It's so nice to see you here again…'

He could see that Milla was finally catching on, picking up the subtext in Lily's gently enquiring tone. He intervened quickly. 'Milla was sketching down by the loch. I asked her in for coffee before she goes back to Strathburn.'

Lily met his gaze for the first time. 'I see.'

'They're lovely flowers.' Milla was trying to change the subject.

'The wedding florist had some extras. I thought they'd look nice in the hall—a splash of colour for our guests.' Lily lifted the vase off the table. 'I'll be back in a moment.'

As soon as she'd gone Milla rushed to his side. 'Does she know?'

'Yes. I'll have to remember to thank Rosie for her discretion.'

Milla's eyes widened. 'She probably didn't mean— Are you okay?'

He nodded and reached for her hand, chafing her fingers gently in his. He wondered, after all, if it would be easier to go with the flow than to hide in the shadows.

He was still thinking about it when the door swung open and his mother came back in. He released Milla's hand instantly, but saw the tell-tale creases forming in Lily's cheeks as, with brisk movements, she started clearing the table of debris from her flower arranging.

'Do you know, I've just been wondering…?' She looked up, a smile finally breaking across her features. 'Milla, would you like to come to the wedding tomorrow?'

He hadn't seen it coming, and it was obvious that Milla hadn't either; words were pouring from her mouth in a rapid stream.

'Oh, no... I couldn't possibly... I mean, it's very kind of you to invite me, but I have a lot to do and—'

'You should come.'

The sound of his own voice shocked him. He felt two pairs of eyes swivel in his direction. He glanced at Lily. She'd blindsided him with her well-meaning gesture, forced him out of the shadows, but maybe it was okay.

He looked into Milla's face. 'I can guarantee that it'll be a great wedding.'

He watched her brow wrinkling in a question. 'I— Do you want me to come?'

He wanted to pull her close and kiss her, but instead he nodded. 'Yes, I do.'

Her eyes misted over, then she broke away from his gaze and turned to Lily. 'I'm flattered to be asked, and actually I would love to come, but there's a tiny problem. I've got nothing to wear that's suitable for a wedding. I mean, walking boots just won't cut it, will they?'

The issue of what to wear would be resolved easily, Lily declared, courtesy of Rosie's overflowing wardrobe.

'You're a similar size. I'm sure we'll find something beautiful. What's your shoe size?'

'Five and a half.'

'That's Rosie's size!' Lily was beaming. 'This was clearly meant to be. After we've had our coffee we'll go get you fitted out. I know you'll look perfect.'

Milla swallowed the last of her misgivings and allowed herself to feel a little excitement. An invitation to Rosie's wedding wasn't exactly what she'd been expecting, but if Cormac wanted her there then that was reason enough to go.

He'd looked so happy when she'd accepted, and the more she thought about it, the more enthusiastic she became. She could tell it was going to be a beautiful wedding. A marquee by the loch, lights in the trees, champagne, a traditional *ceilidh*, and most importantly Cormac at her side.

She caught his eye as he spooned coffee into a large cafetière and blushed at the heat she saw in his gaze.

She turned her attention back to Lily. 'Well, as long as Rosie won't mind lending me something—'

'Of course she won't mind—'

'Won't mind what?' Rosie had come through the door, an envelope in her hand.

'You won't mind lending Milla something to wear for tomorrow.' Lily smiled. 'She's coming to the wedding!'

'How fantastic!' Rosie's eyes darted to Cormac, her lips twitching in amusement, then she turned to Milla and smiled warmly. 'I'm so glad you're going to join us, and of course I don't mind lending you something.'

Cormac slotted the lid onto the coffee pot. 'I don't remember you being so happy when I said *I* was coming.' He reached into a cupboard for mugs.

'You were a sure thing—but if you need to hear it, I *am* delighted that you're here…'

She worked her finger into the flap of the envelope she was holding and pulled out a slim white card. Milla watched as her face lit up all over again.

'Oh, my goodness. You'll never guess what… Emma's coming to the wedding after all.'

There was a loud clatter as two of the mugs fell onto the worktop. Cormac muttered an apology, but Rosie and Lily carried on talking as if they hadn't noticed. Milla studied Cormac's back as he made the coffee, noticed the sudden tension in his shoulders. She tried to catch his eye, but he seemed intent on his task. Perplexed, she refocused on what Rosie and Lily were saying.

'That *is* good news.' Lily smiled. 'It will be lovely to see her.' She caught Milla's eye. 'Emma's a friend of the family. She's...' She raked the air for words. 'A good friend. We thought she might not be able to make it.'

Milla saw Rosie fire a warning look at Lily, and there was a moment of awkward silence as Cormac brought the mugs to the table. He didn't look at her and she felt that it was deliberate.

Puzzled, she tried again to catch his eye, but he was lifting his coffee and walking towards the door. 'They need me outside, so I'll go get on. Please excuse me.'

Without a backward glance he left the room.

Rosie pulled open the doors of a wide mahogany wardrobe and rummaged through the hangers, pulling out garments and hanging them along the top rail.

'Just shout out if you see anything you like.'

Milla sat on the bed, feeling wretched. She couldn't wipe away the image of Cormac's averted gaze as he'd set her coffee mug down, the casual indifference in his manner as he'd left the kitchen without so much as a glance in her direction. She'd wanted to go after him but it had been impossible to extricate herself, and now she was trapped again.

Those mugs had fallen from his hands and

bounced on the worktop. Cormac was physically adept; he wasn't clumsy. He'd cursed under his breath, but she'd sensed that his frustration had nothing to do with dropping the mugs.

What had she told him days ago? *'You can always see more; you just have to open your eyes a little wider, that's all.'*

As Rosie pulled out dress after dress Milla forced her eyes to open a little wider. Someone called Emma was coming to the wedding. Rosie and Lily were pleased, but Cormac had dropped the coffee mugs.

'So, what do you think?' Rosie was holding up a silk chiffon dress in a shade of *eau-de-nil*.

Milla eased herself off the bed and stepped closer. 'It's beautiful.'

Rosie was examining the label. 'It's still got the tags on—it's never been worn.' She held it out at arm's length and frowned. 'I think I bought it for a charity event but then I got the flu and couldn't go.' She held it up to Milla's frame. 'If it fits, it's going to be perfect.' She smiled. 'Go and try it on.'

Milla took the hanger from her hand and entered the adjoining bathroom. Slowly she pulled her tee shirt over her head and slipped out of her jeans. She checked her fingernails for traces of paint before touching the dress. The fabric was sheer and soft, dauntingly expensive. She stepped into it and pulled up the zip as far as she could; Rosie would have to help her with the rest.

As if sensing that she was needed, Rosie put her head around the door. 'You probably need a hand…'

Milla felt the dress slide into its proper place across her back and shoulders as Rosie carefully eased up the zip and then stood back.

'Wow! You look stunning—Cor's going to die when he sees you—sorry! That just slipped out… I hope you don't think—'

'It's fine. Don't worry about it.'

Milla turned to look in the mirror and caught her breath. The dress was exquisite, with soft folds of silk chiffon spilling from a fitted bodice. The neckline was high, slashed in a wide curve across her collarbones and resolving into neat cap sleeves perched on her shoulders. It could have been made for her.

She resisted a girlish impulse to swish the skirt. 'Oh, Rosie, it's beautiful.'

'Shoes! I bought matching shoes and never wore those either.'

Rosie skipped out of the bathroom to retrieve them. Milla stared at her reflection. Would Cormac 'die' when he saw her? She attempted a smile, but it wouldn't come. Something about the way he'd left so quickly…

'Here you are.' Rosie reappeared, brandishing a pair of elegant two-tone heels in cream and *eau-de-nil*, silk bows with diamanté on their toes.

Milla slipped them on, felt the unfamiliar surge in height. She tried a hesitant step or two.

Rosie regarded her with interest. 'How do they feel?'

'They make me feel like someone else,' she said, and then, in case Rosie took offence, she added quickly, 'But in a good way.' She shifted her weight backwards and forwards, trying to get used to the unfamiliar sensation. 'Can I ask you something?'

'Of course.'

'Who's Emma?'

Rosie sucked in a low breath. 'Ah…that ever so slightly awkward moment didn't get past you, then…'

'I wondered if I was imagining it…'

'You weren't.' She frowned. 'Has Cormac told you what happened in Afghanistan?'

'Yes.'

'Well, that's progress, anyway.' She sighed and cast her eyes to the ceiling. 'Mentioning Duncan in front of Cormac, or anything connected with Duncan, is a bit like talking about Lord Voldemort—*he who shall not be named* and all that.'

Milla felt her brow wrinkle. 'Okay, but I still don't understand. Who is Emma?'

Rosie stood up and eased down the zip of Milla's dress. 'Emma is—or perhaps I should say *was*—Duncan's wife. You saw how Cor reacted just now? We all loved Duncan, but he just can't get over it. They were friends—I'd have thought he'd be pleased to see her.'

Rosie seemed to be contemplating something, then she smiled at Milla's reflection in the mirror.

'Look, we're having a little pre-wedding party tonight—all the nearest and dearest. I think you should come. You're good for Cormac, and I think he'd like you to be there. You could stay the night and then you'll already be here for the wedding.'

Milla was about to protest, but Rosie stopped her with a smile.

'We won't tell him—it'll be a nice surprise. I've even got the perfect little black dress for you to wear…'

Milla laid the garment bag and shoes on the back seat of the four-by-four and closed the door. How effortlessly she'd been woven into Rosie's wedding plans—and now she was to make a surprise appearance at the pre-wedding *soirée*. Rosie was so excited about the whole thing that Milla had found it impossible to refuse, but now, as she looked around for signs of Cormac, she felt an overwhelming desire to run a million miles in the opposite direction. She was troubled by that scene in the kitchen. Perplexed at the way he'd avoided her gaze before disappearing.

The stretch of driveway closest to the marquee was filling up with a growing assortment of vehicles—a compact yellow van with a livery of scrolling letters circling a wedding cake, a larger square van with the doors thrown back, two cheery ladies decanting an assortment of large letters spelling out the word LOVE.

She set off across the lawn in the direction of the marquee in case he was there. Rosie seemed to think that any mention of Duncan was enough to throw her brother into a tailspin, and that his reaction to Emma's acceptance of the wedding invitation was simply part of that, but she wasn't so sure. She needed to see him. Find out what was going on.

The marquee's interior was soft with milky light. The air was filled with the sweet, earthy aroma of damp grass overlaid with fragrant notes of the narcissi and hyacinth from the floral centrepieces being set out on circular tables by a short, lively girl. At the far end another girl was tying hessian bows to the backs of chevalier chairs while she chatted to a colleague.

There was no sign of Cormac.

She turned to leave—and walked straight into a large cardboard box being carried into the marquee by another girl. A dismal clash and tinkle caused the florist and the venue stylist to look up, and Milla felt a hot rush of embarrassment.

'I'm so sorry. That didn't sound good. Have I broken it, whatever it was?'

The girl steadied herself and tugged the box to rights. 'No. It's fine—it's just the tea light holders, and they're indestructible.'

Relieved, Milla ventured a question. 'I don't suppose you've seen Cormac Buchanan, by any chance…?'

The girl set the box down and pushed her hair away from her face. 'I think he's checking some deliveries behind the caterer's tent.'

'Thanks. And I'm sorry about—'

The girl smiled. 'No worries.'

Milla stepped out of the marquee and drew a steadying breath. Crashing into the box of tea light holders had shredded her nerves even more. All she needed was to look into his eyes and then she'd know that everything was all right.

Around the back there was an assortment of

smaller tents, a tangle of cabling and a grumbling generator. She picked her way carefully through the maze and finally found him in a forest of wine crates, signing off on a delivery. She was about to call out when Sam's head popped up from behind another stack of boxes.

'How many cases of the Pinot Noir should we have?'

Cormac flipped over a sheet on the clipboard in his hand and ran a pen down a row of figures. 'I think it's...'

She stepped backwards out of sight, then retraced her steps. He was busy, and she couldn't talk to him about Emma while Sam was there. She'd go back to the bothy and get on with Rosie's painting. She'd talk to him later.

Despite her misgivings, she felt a smile tug at the corners of her mouth. The black dress Rosie had given her was exquisite. He'd only ever seen her in her work clothes. Tonight he'd get the surprise of his life and she couldn't wait to see his face.

CHAPTER TEN

CORMAC WORKED HIS tie into a Windsor knot and stared at his reflection with unseeing eyes. This morning he'd told Milla that wild horses wouldn't stop him from seeing her today. He'd told her he wanted her to come to the wedding, and when he'd said it he'd meant it, but now everything had changed.

He'd spent the day in purgatory, trying to think of another way, but he couldn't dodge his miserable errand any longer. If Emma was coming to the wedding, then Milla couldn't be there. How could he walk into the wedding reception with a beautiful girl on his arm when Emma was all alone? It would be like flaunting his happiness, shouting from the rooftops that he was done with grieving and had moved on with his life.

He'd never escape this guilt. He could see now that it was always going to be this way—catching him out, nipping at his heels. He'd lowered his defences, started to believe that he could have a relationship with someone, but he'd been a fool. This time he'd dropped some mugs; next time it could be something far worse. He couldn't burden Milla with his erratic moods, his nightmares, his fear. It would be better for everyone if he was alone.

He glanced at his watch. If he left now, he could make it to the bothy and back before anyone missed him—it would only take him a few moments to tell Milla that it was never going to work between them and then he'd be free. Broken-hearted, but free.

On the landing, he hesitated. He could already hear the hum of voices downstairs, the musicians tuning their instruments. He had no idea how he was going to get through the evening. After he'd seen Milla he knew he wouldn't want to come back—he'd rather go to a bar and get drunk—but his family would never forgive him and so he was trapped. He'd have to play the part of the dutiful Calcarron heir, endure it somehow.

He forced his legs to move forward, and was halfway down the stairs when he froze mid-step, mesmerised, tongue-tied and bewildered. Milla had stepped out of the drawing room and was looking up at him, a shy smile on her lips. He felt his eyes clouding. He'd never seen her like this—elegant in a black dress and stilettoes, her hair swept up in a diamanté clasp.

Before he had time to collect his thoughts, Rosie skipped into the hall, giggling.

'We thought we'd surprise you.' She slid an arm around Milla's waist. 'Doesn't she look gorgeous?'

He could hardly summon the breath to speak. 'Yes.'

Milla's eyes were searching his, and he couldn't bear the flicker of confusion he could see there. His collar suddenly felt too tight. They'd planned this and blown him out of the water. As he descended the final steps he was seized with bitterness. Why did she have to look so irresistible?

With difficulty he met her wounded gaze. 'You look beautiful. I never expected—'

'That's the beauty of surprises, Cor. You're not meant to expect them.' Rosie squeezed his shoulder and motioned to an overnight bag parked on a chair. 'I insisted that Milla should stay tonight—it'll make it so much easier for the wedding tomorrow.' She leaned in to kiss his cheek and whispered, 'You can thank me later.' She stepped back and smiled. 'I'll leave you two to say a proper hello.' She threw him a playful glance and disappeared into the drawing room.

For a moment, he stood in a kind of daze.

'You look very handsome.'

Milla's faltering smile made him feel even worse and, desperate to escape, he reached for her bag.

'Thank you. I'll take this up for you.'

He started up the stairs and knew immediately that she was following. Behind him, he could feel her anguish shimmering through the air along with her perfume, could hear her bottled silence straining at the cork.

As he neared his own room he hesitated, then walked past, turned a corner and led her to the room she'd used before. Perhaps it was a good thing she was following, because at least they'd have a few moments alone. It would have been easier to say what he had to say at the bothy, but now he had no choice. He'd have to do it here.

After she'd gone he'd tell Rosie she hadn't been feeling well and had decided to go back to Strathburn.

He closed the door behind them and opened his mouth to speak, but she spoke first.

'What's wrong, Cormac? If I've done something wrong you've got help me out, because I have no idea what's going on in your head right now.'

Her eyes were wide with incomprehension and the trembling hurt choking her voice almost shattered his defences.

'Rosie said it would be fun to surprise you, but I'm sensing you're not seeing it that way.'

'It was a shock, that's all.' He felt the muscles tighten in his jaw. 'I—I was actually on my way to see you...'

Her eyes softened, and her voice steadied with relief. 'You were coming to see me?' She stepped towards him, her lips curving into a smile. 'Well, I'm here, dressed to the nines, just for you.'

One of her shoulders was bare, the skin smooth and milky. It was all he could do not to reach out and touch her. He swallowed hard.

'I was coming to tell you that you can't come to the wedding tomorrow.'

Her voice was a broken hush. 'Why?'

He blanked his gaze. 'I changed my mind.'

Incredulity mangled her voice. 'You changed your mind...? Just like that?' She was shaking her head, her eyes suddenly steely. 'That's not good enough. I need an explanation.'

He might have guessed she'd pursue him, make him twist the knife.

He masked his shrivelling heart with a shrug. 'I don't want to give you the wrong impression—about us. About where this is going.'

She recoiled, her gaze seeming to turn inwards. 'Am I so easy to cast aside? What's happened to you? I don't recognise you any more.'

He looked down at his feet—anywhere was better than her eyes. 'I told you before; I'm a screw-up. I'm unreliable.'

He watched her eyes fill with indignant fury. She squared herself in front of him, her hands balled into fists.

'How dare you?' She spat out the words. 'How dare you hide behind all that?' Her eyes were gleaming with tears now. 'I don't know what's going on, but I know you're lying. You're lying to me, but worst of all you're lying to yourself.' She walked to the door and turned. 'It's a pity. I thought you were someone I could love. I thought that behind the tortured silences and the wounded eyes there might be something worth treasuring—'

A knock on the door shocked her to silence and she turned away quickly to wipe the tears from her eyes. He ran a hand through his hair, drew in a ragged breath. He'd hurt her, and she'd hurt him right back. This was exactly the wrong moment for an interruption.

He checked to see that she'd composed herself, then reached for the handle.

'Here you are!' Sam grinned at Milla. 'Wow! You look gorgeous.' He stepped forward and kissed her on both cheeks.

She seemed to melt into Sam's embrace, then

stood away, a dazzling smile on her lips. 'And you look very handsome.'

Cormac felt a muscle twitch in his jaw and rubbed at it in irritation. 'Sam, can you give us a minute, please?'

'Sure. But you're wanted downstairs. I was sent to fetch you.'

'I'll be right down.'

He looked at Milla and she returned his gaze with an unfamiliar glint of calculation. Then she stepped forward and slid her arm through Sam's.

'It's fine. I think we're done here anyway, and after such a *kind* invitation to the party I certainly don't want to keep everyone waiting. Shall we go?'

Milla was smiling but her heart was breaking. She didn't understand what was going on in Cormac's head and she didn't understand herself either. What had possessed her to take Sam's arm? She'd been about to run away and now she was walking down the stairs to a party she had no wish to attend.

For an instant the thought of torturing Cormac with her presence for the rest of the evening had seemed like fitting payback for the hurt he'd caused, but she was already regretting it. She'd always heard that revenge was a dish best served cold, and now she knew it was true.

This morning at the loch he'd turned her inside out with his kiss. That had been real. Not this. Why had he changed? The words that had just fallen from his mouth sounded like the lines from some corny movie. She could have handled the truth—whatever it was—but he'd delivered his speech and then tossed her aside, just like Dan had.

She felt the tears gathering again and forced them back. Crying wouldn't solve anything; she had to think straight.

In the grand hall a waiter handed them crystal flutes of champagne, then Sam disappeared through the crowd of guests to greet an aunt and uncle. Milla could feel Cormac behind her as she entered the large drawing room. It had been transformed for the party, with tall candelabras and exquisite floral arrangements. From the far end of the room, she could hear a violin playing Vivaldi, but the music gave her no comfort.

She took a mouthful of champagne, and then another, feeling its cold fizz quickly dulling the edges of her pain. At her side, Cormac seemed to be locked into a brooding silence, and she wondered what she should do. Cut loose at the earliest opportunity or take him aside, try to make him explain…?

She looked at him briefly. Maybe she should back off altogether. He'd hurt her twice in as many days and she wasn't sure she could stand any more heartache, or any more uncertainty. She was a girl who circled maps, a girl who wanted to know where she was going, and he seemed so lost that he couldn't even find a map.

When curious eyes turned towards them, he shifted restlessly. 'I need to mingle and you're going to have to come with me.'

He guided her into the room, stopping only to hand her a fresh glass from a passing tray. There followed a succession of formal introductions to his family, the groom's family, and a select group of friends. She noticed that he introduced her as a talented artist—an effective way of diverting the conversation into art and away from any enquiries about their relationship.

She found that by concentrating on everyone else she could almost forget about Cormac, so she sipped her champagne and chatted with the guests. Somehow she remembered their names and managed to look interested in everything they said. She felt warmth and admiration in their eyes—and then she realised that, far from forgetting about Cormac, she had designed her every move to draw his attention, *his* admiration.

When he steered her into a quiet spot near

the fireplace she thought he was going to tell her he was sorry for what he'd said upstairs, but instead he whispered, 'Why didn't you just leave, Milla?'

His words stung, and she understood finally that there was no point in trying to win his admiration. He didn't want her. She felt a sob building in her chest and choked it back. She'd leave first thing in the morning, but if she had to go she'd make sure she took her dignity with her.

She lifted her chin and met his gaze. 'I'm not sure. I *was* thinking of leaving, but then I changed my mind. I suppose I'm rather flaky— you know, unreliable... But I'm sure *you* understand that better than anyone.'

She felt the biting whiplash of her own sarcasm and couldn't meet his eye again. When she saw Rosie beckoning her over she was relieved.

She imagined his eyes burning into her back as she made her way across the room in her borrowed dress and shoes. When she'd been getting ready for the party she'd been excited to see his reaction. How deflated she'd felt when he'd gazed at her from the landing. The entire evening had been a miserable charade and now he'd driven her to this bitter mudslinging when the truth was that she didn't want to hurt him at all. She was in love with him.

Suddenly she tripped over her own thought…
He'd driven her to mud-slinging.

Seized by a moment of clarity, she looked back and found herself staring straight into his eyes. In the split-second before his gaze hardened she saw everything.

'I'm not what you need, Milla. I don't want you to care about me because I'll only let you down, like I let Duncan down.'

He'd said those words to her yesterday, before the storm broke. That was the truth. He wasn't rejecting her—he was driving her away for some other reason.

As she turned away from his gaze she was overtaken with compassion for the man she loved. It wasn't about herself any more. If she could work out why he was pushing her away, then maybe she could help him.

When she reached Rosie's side, the girl leaned into her ear. 'Cormac can't take his eyes off you. I knew he'd love it if you came tonight.' She smiled and motioned to a dark-haired young man with intense blue eyes. 'Now, I'd like to introduce you to Fraser's friend Connor. Not only is he one of the groomsmen, he also writes for the *Art Review*.'

Cormac glanced at his watch. How much longer would he have to endure this torture? He'd done the rounds, made polite conversation with Fraser's family, and now he'd been drawn into a group discussing the demerits of a proposed wind farm. As the heir to Calcarron it was his duty to mingle, but he was finding it increasingly difficult to focus.

He sipped his drink without tasting it and watched Milla out of the corner of his eye. He was fully aware that he'd driven her to staging this ridiculous side-show. That she would put him through this was a measure of how much he'd hurt her, and the pain of that knowledge was tearing him apart. The dress, her hair— she'd taken so much trouble for him and he hadn't even kissed her cheek.

Clearly Rosie had introduced Milla to Connor Lawson because of his connections with the *Art Review*, but it was hard to watch Connor wielding his exaggerated charm—all that leaning in, the meaty hand pawing at her arm.

Milla looked as if she was concentrating hard on what he was telling her—maybe a little too hard. Could she feel his eyes on her from across the room? He could see that little crease she got between her eyes when she was paying attention. He'd kissed her there this morning, when she'd been trying to show him a shading technique.

His heart buckled in his chest. Why was he

tormenting himself like this? He shifted his gaze and Rosie caught his eye. She started making her way towards him, but he couldn't cope with his sister right now. He excused himself politely, put down his glass and strode out of the room.

Outside, the light was fading. Bats darted through the gloaming, feeding on midges and clumsy moths. He loosened his tie and walked across the lawn towards the loch. At the end of the short jetty where the skiff was moored he sat down and kicked his legs over the side. He felt the soft breeze against his face, heard the slop of water against the boat and wondered how he was going to get through the next twenty-four hours.

'Cormac!'

Milla's voice shocked him to his feet and turned his mouth to dust. He watched dumbly as she slipped off her shoes, bent to pick them up and walked slowly along the jetty towards him. He noticed the breeze rippling the soft folds of her dress around her bare legs as she moved and for a moment he was lost.

She stopped in front of him and lifted her eyes to his face. She held his gaze for a few moments then moistened her lips. 'It's been a strange week, don't you think?'

He nodded slowly, not daring to speak. He

could see the glimmer of tears at the corners of her eyes, but there was no tremble in her voice, no bitterness.

She gestured to the marquee on the lawn behind them. 'It's going to be a beautiful wedding tomorrow. I hope you all have a wonderful day.'

He felt a twist of anguish and let his gaze fall to her feet, smooth and pale on the wooden boards.

She stepped around him and sat down at the edge of the jetty, hugging her knees. 'Will you sit with me for a while?' He didn't know what she was trying to do, but for some reason he couldn't walk away. He dropped down beside her and looked across the water. He could feel her eyes on his face, gently watchful.

'How are you feeling about tomorrow?'

Finally he found his voice. He lifted an eyebrow and attempted a smile. 'I'm confident that the marquee won't fall down, that the lighting will look awesome, and I'm pretty sure that there'll be enough champagne.'

'I wasn't talking about that.'

He pressed his lips into a line and gazed across the water. 'What, then?'

'I was talking about Emma. You dropped the coffee mugs when Rosie read out that acceptance card.'

So she'd noticed after all. It was no surprise.

He'd felt her eyes on him in the kitchen but he hadn't trusted himself to look at her, and he couldn't look at her now. He didn't want to talk about this.

He made a move to get up and felt her hand on his arm.

'Please stay, Cor. Rosie's been telling me how you shut yourself down every time anyone tries to talk to you about Duncan, but you've got to get past it. It wasn't your fault—can't you see that? Emma doesn't blame you for what happened, so you've got to stop blaming yourself.'

He hadn't expected her to talk like this. He'd been expecting another bitter admonishment, and now the concern in her voice was tearing him apart.

He dropped his head into his hands. 'I can't.'

His head was filled with noise and blur. He could hear the whine of gunfire, see Duncan being ripped off the bridge in a splatter of blood. He was crawling through the sand, calling Duncan's name, sobbing, praying under his breath, heart hammering, bowels struggling. Then he found him. But it wasn't Duncan any more. Just a glistening mess of flesh and splintered bone. There'd been an endless, ludicrous moment of denial and then the dark drop of realisation, retching through a howl of pain.

He swallowed hard, watched the ebbing and

bobbing of the waves on the water. 'No one understands. The last time my family saw Duncan it was here, before we went to Afghanistan. We were all here together that weekend—Duncan and Emma, Rosie and Fraser, Sam.'

He felt the ghost of a smile forming on his lips.

'We were fooling around on that skiff—pushing each other into the loch, having fun. We lit a fire over there on the beach—Sam toasted marshmallows and we had a few drinks. Happy memories.'

He turned to face her.

'Maybe it's easier if your last memory of someone is a happy one, but I don't have that. When I close my eyes I see things I don't want to see, and I remember that it should have been me on that bridge.' He ran a hand through his hair. 'I used to go and see Emma and the baby, but the way she'd look at me sometimes... I couldn't stand it. If guilt is dragging me down then I'm sorry, but that's the way it is and I can't do anything about it.'

'So you're going to spend your whole life in mourning? You think Duncan would want that? Do you think that's what Emma wants?'

He stared at the water.

'You can hide behind your silence if you like, but while you're clinging to your grief you need to know that your family is grieving as well.'

He heard a catch in her voice and looked up.
'They lost you that day too, and they want
you back.' Her eyes were glistening. 'I know
how hard it is to see someone you love die, but I
think it's even harder to watch a person you love
dying because they've forgotten how to live.'

She wiped her tears away with slender fingers.

'Emma's coming to the wedding and I think
you're scared. I don't know anything about her,
but I think that if she's brave enough to face the
world again then she'll be happy to think that
you can do the same.'

He wished she would stop talking. Her words
were turning him inside out, stealing the air
from his lungs. A swell of tears filled his eyes,
but he couldn't make his lips form the words
he wanted to say.

She held his gaze for a few moments, then
rose to her feet, shoes dangling in her hands. 'I
love you, Cor, but I'm leaving in the morning
because I can't compete with Duncan's memory
and it's hurting me too much to try.'

He heard the soft pad of her feet on the
wooden boards behind him, then her faltering
step. He twisted round to look at her as the scent
of her perfume reached him on the breeze.

'I finished Rosie's painting this afternoon.

I'll leave it in the bothy for you. It'll be dry by tomorrow. Goodbye, Cormac.'

She turned away and walked to the end of the jetty, then disappeared into the gloom.

After she'd gone he watched the last silver glow receding behind the mountains. She'd come out here asking nothing for herself. Interceding on behalf of his family, trying to help him see sense—and she was right about everything.

He closed his eyes, forced himself to picture Duncan's face at the campfire, laughing and cursing as a toasted marshmallow slid off the skewer and exploded in his lap. Running and jumping off the jetty—always trying to go faster and further than anyone else. If there was a way forward it had to be through remembering the good times, and there'd been so many good times.

His brain fumbled as Milla's face shimmered into his thoughts. He'd known her for a matter of days, and already there was so much good.

He pictured her teasing eyes by the roadside, her delight when she'd stepped into the bothy for the first time, the feel of her hair against his cheek as he'd carried her along the path, the crazy safari they'd taken so she could draw, the way she'd tried to hide behind the menu in the restaurant, the way she'd kissed him under the

Northern Lights, the way she'd listened when he told her about Duncan, the way she'd dried his body after the rain.

The way she'd drawn his face—captured the sadness in his eyes.

He'd been an idiot. If he'd explained why the news that Emma was coming to the wedding had thrown him into a flat spin she would have understood. Instead he'd tried to shut her out, but she'd come here to talk to him anyway.

A spark of hope flickered to fullness in his heart and suddenly he wondered why he was still sitting there.

He jumped to his feet and strode down the jetty onto the lawn. She'd said she was leaving tomorrow, which meant she was still here to-night.

He broke into a run.

In her room, Milla clicked on a low light, then took off Rosie's dress and slipped it onto a hanger. She paired the shoes and parked them under the bedroom chair. She pulled on her robe and sat on the edge of the bed, waiting for her tears to come.

She'd known Cormac was lying about why he didn't want her to come to the wedding, and as Connor had droned on and on in the draw-ing room she'd worked it all out.

The words he'd spoken that morning had come back to her: *'I don't want us to be the centre of attention.'*

She'd realised that his guilt about Duncan would never have permitted him to look happy in front of Emma, to have someone with him at the wedding. If he was alone he could be respectfully unobtrusive. He'd sacrificed Milla on the altar of his guilt—given her up for Emma's sake.

She shivered and pulled her robe tighter. He'd tried to hide behind clichés—he'd called himself a screw-up. The sad truth was that he was right—but not in the way he'd meant.

When she'd finally extricated herself from Connor Rosie had taken her aside and told her how worried she was about Cormac, how desperately she wanted her brother back. At that moment she'd decided to go and find him. His perspective was skewed, and unless that changed he would never heal, never be able to love someone.

She'd tried so hard to get through to him, but she'd failed.

Tomorrow she'd leave early, get her things from the bothy and go back to London. She'd never cope with seeing him again because he hadn't put out a hand to stop her. He'd let her walk away.

She felt a tear rolling down her cheek and wiped it away with the back of her hand. She loved him. She loved this place. It would be hard to go.

A gentle knocking startled her. She crossed to open the door, expecting it to be Rosie, but it was Cormac who was standing in the hallway. He was slightly breathless, as if he'd been running, and his eyes were burning with something that looked like hope.

She felt a little wrench inside her chest.

He stepped towards her. 'I saw your light on. May I come in?'

His top button was undone, his tie loosened against the crisp white shirt. She moistened her lips and nodded slowly, standing back for him to enter.

Inside, he turned to face her. 'I'm sorry.'

She noticed the tension in his shoulders, heard the hitch in his breath.

A bubble of emotion churned inside her, turning her words into a whisper. 'You're sorry…?'

He took a tentative step towards her, licked his lips quickly. 'I could say a lot more, and if you're happy to give me the time of day then I will, but straight off the bat I thought "sorry" would cover all the bases.'

She felt a smile forming on her lips, a little spark glowing in her heart. 'It's a good opener, but I'm not sure about giving you the time of day when we've got all night. I'd rather hear it now.'

He stepped closer and she felt the chaos of sensation she always felt when he was near.

'My head's a mess, and it'll probably all come out as a jumble, but what you said at the jetty—you were right.'

He closed his eyes briefly, shook his head in self-admonishment.

'I thought that letting you in, living any kind of life for myself, was like letting Duncan go—and that felt like the ultimate betrayal. I didn't want Emma to see us together, to see how happy you make me. I didn't want her to think I'd moved on and left her behind in her grief. But you've made me see that I can't go on like that. I've been sinking for so long that I didn't even know I was drowning.'

He reached a hand to her face and the warmth of his fingers made her head reel.

'You threw me a lifeline, pulled me back to the surface, and even though I've been kicking and screaming the whole time, now that I'm here I don't want to sink again. I know it won't be easy, but I need you, Milla. Will you keep me afloat?'

Her eyes burned with hot tears—he wasn't lost to her after all.

She slipped her hands to his waist, felt the delicious heat of his body radiating through his shirt. 'What makes you think that you even had to ask?'

He smiled slowly, his eyes glowing with a light that made the breath catch in her throat.

'Maybe I did do something right, way back in time—something to deserve you.'

She slid her hands over his chest, pulled his tie free of its knot. 'I think you should stop talking now.'

He laughed softly and took her face into his hands. 'As usual, you're absolutely right.'

CHAPTER ELEVEN

CORMAC STIRRED AND shifted across the pillow, so he could feel her hair against his cheek. He loved waking up beside her—the warmth of her body, the scent of her hair. It was delicious, like herbs and apples.

He closed his eyes and felt a wave of happiness wash over him. During the night he'd woken up with an idea and he needed her unbiased opinion. He glanced at the clock on the bedside table. It was early enough for them to escape without being seen, and they'd be back long before they needed to get ready for the wedding.

She *would* be coming to the wedding. It might feel awkward for a few moments, but after everything he'd been through he could brave a few awkward moments.

He pressed his lips to her hair. 'Milla! Wake up. We need to go.'

She snuggled into his arms and groaned. 'Need to go where?'

'Outside. I want to show you something.'

She lifted her face and he kissed her softly.

'Come on—get dressed. Jeans and walking boots. I'll see you downstairs and don't make a sound. If we're spotted, we're done for.'

The large door creaked as he led her out into the cool breath of dawn. It was a calm day, with a gentle warmth filtering through a haze of cloud which would burn off as the sun ripened. He tugged her, giggling, across the drive to where his sports car was parked and motioned for her to get in. Then he put his backpack into the compact boot, let the top down and slipped into the driver's seat.

'Ready?'

She eyed him in amusement. 'Ready as I'll ever be at stupid o'clock in the morning.'

He laughed and turned the key in the ignition. 'It'll be worth it—you'll see.'

He smiled as she settled herself into the plush leather seat, let her head fall back against the head rest. He needed this time alone with her before the bustle and excitement of the wedding and he loved early mornings, when possibilities hung in the air like drops of dew.

He drove through Ardoig and followed the road which wound over the estate in the other direction. He felt her eyes on him as he negotiated a bend.

'You're a very handsome person, Cormac Buchanan. Have I told you that?'

He laughed. 'No.' He glanced at her, saw a smile hovering on her lips.

'I was most likely saving it for a special occasion.'

His eyebrow lifted. 'Is that what this is?'

She reached a hand to the back of his neck and smiled. 'Maybe.'

After another bend the road straightened out, and he accelerated through a deserted tract of wild moorland. Black scars of peat ripped through the fabric of the landscape while silver rocks burst randomly through the heather in craggy peaks. The rising sun bloomed through the thinning cloud, throwing down slanting golden rays.

He squinted at Milla's face. She was taking it all in, her eyes wide. 'What do you think of the view?'

She didn't turn to look at him. 'It's inspiring. If I'd brought my sketchbook I'd be asking you to pull over.'

He smiled to himself, tapped his fingers on the steering wheel. It was exactly what he'd wanted to hear. He drove on, slowing for bends as the road wound upwards, twisting and turning until it crested the hill.

In a lay-by, he pulled in and turned off the engine. 'We're here. Come on.'

'Come on?' She surveyed the wilderness in confusion. 'Come on where?'

She got out of the car and waited while he shouldered the rucksack.

'It's not far; just a short hike.'

She rose on her tiptoes and kissed him quickly. 'Lead on—I'll be right behind.'

For a while they tromped along the path with sturdy stems of heather brushing against their legs. When he suddenly realised that he could only hear his own footsteps he swung round, perplexed. She wasn't there.

With a thumping heart he scanned the path, then started to run back the way he'd come. 'Milla! Mill—'

A strangled giggle close by stopped him in his tracks, and within seconds he found her lying behind a clump of heather, buckled up with laughter.

He jumped on top of her and pinned her hands over her head playfully. 'That wasn't very nice. I thought I'd lost you.'

She stopped laughing and eyed him mischievously. 'You were going too fast for me—you said this was going to be a short hike, not a forced march. I'm recovering from an injury, remember?'

Her voice was husky from laughing, her chest rising and falling softly in panting breaths, and for a moment he was mesmerised. He released her hands and instantly she wound her arms around his neck, pulling his mouth to hers.

It was too easy to get lost in her kisses, the feel of her body beneath him, and it was all he could do to tear himself away.

'Come on—we need to get going.' He got to his feet and pulled her up beside him. 'You lead the way this time—a good commander always marches at the pace of the slowest. Stay on this track and keep going.'

At the edge of a ridge, Milla stopped.

He wrapped his arms around her and she sank back against him. He nuzzled her neck. 'What do you think of this view?'

She looked up into his face. 'Frankly? I'm miffed. I don't have a sketchbook with me and this is too wonderful not to draw.'

He kissed her. 'Tell me what's wonderful about it, exactly?'

She looked at him incredulously. 'Can't you see it? This view is alive with texture—the way the light grazes the landscape, the colours of the heather, the grasses, those gashes of peat... If you can't see it you must be blind.'

He laughed. 'I do see it, but I'm not an artist. I like looking at the world through your eyes.'

They walked on. Cormac felt a swell in the air. The day was going to be fine and warm, and he was glad for Rosie's sake.

They reached the top of the hill and their destination came into view. A small stone bothy with a gently pitched slate roof.

As they made their final approach he watched Milla's brow crinkle in confusion. 'Who'd live here? It's miles from anywhere.'

He worked the handle back and forth, then gave the door a shove. 'It's not for living in; this is a real bothy—a place for shepherds and walkers to shelter from bad weather.'

He ducked his head and entered the gloomy space, slipping his backpack onto an ancient trestle table.

She followed him inside. 'So why have you brought me here?'

'Because I wanted you to see it.'

She spun round slowly on her heel and lifted an eyebrow. 'It would be an understatement to say that this place needs work.' She crossed back to the door and looked out. 'It's a lovely view, right enough…'

'That's all I needed to know. I brought breakfast—bacon rolls and coffee.'

She turned, a small smile playing on her lips. 'That was an inspired decision.'

He poured two coffees from a flask and

handed her a roll wrapped in foil. The early sun was already warming the bothy wall. They sat with their backs to the stone and watched a dainty grey partridge picking its way through the grass.

He leaned across to kiss her hair. 'So, you wish you'd brought your sketchbook today?'

'Yes! I think I'll need to come back soon—tomorrow, maybe.'

He sipped his coffee and smiled. Her enthusiasm was like an endorsement of everything he'd been thinking. 'We can come back tomorrow if you want.'

She was gazing at him, a bemused expression on her face. 'You're looking mighty pleased with yourself. Are you going to tell me what's going on?'

He wondered what she could see in his eyes. Could she see that he was head over heels in love with her?

It felt too soon to say it, so he smiled. 'Later, maybe. Right now I need this bacon roll.'

Her eyes narrowed, her lips curving upwards into a smile. 'You make a very good bacon roll.'

He laughed and shrugged. 'Nothing to do with me—I charmed one of the caterers.'

Cormac gazed over Loch Calcarron, taking in its timeless beauty, inhaling its freshwater scent.

He could hear the distant creak and slam of doors as wedding guests got out of their cars. He could hear exclamations of delight and the happy laughter of reunions.

He looked across the glinting chop of waves and thought about Duncan. For too long he'd chased his friend away, unable to meet his eye for guilt, but now he invited him into his memory.

You should never have gone over that bridge, Duncan. If only I hadn't taken that call you'd be alive now.

Did he imagine the weight of an arm around his shoulders? A familiar voice in his ear?

But you wouldn't, so now you need to do enough living for both of us. Live it large, Cor. Enjoy every moment.

He drew in a slow breath and blinked moisture from his eyes. He was imagining it, of course. It was all pouring out of him because of Emma. She'd arrived early, to spend a little time with them all. He'd been nervous, but within moments of seeing her his chains had loosened and crashed to the floor.

She was content, she'd said. Shyly she'd told him that she'd met someone, and was worried that he would think badly of her. He'd held her and that was enough. They hadn't needed words to mend their fences.

He'd felt light-headed, strangely euphoric, so he'd escaped to the loch where he'd spent so much time with Duncan. The slopping of the water and the memories of his friend had soothed him.

The sun shouldered its way through the last cloud and threw a burst of warmth onto his face, instantly rearranging the clutter of thoughts in his head. He was caught up in a surge of pure feeling and he smiled as he realised slowly that it was a feeling of happiness.

He took a last long look across the water, then checked his watch.

He needed to speak to his father, and if he hurried he'd have time before the wedding.

Milla relaxed her shoulders and smiled. 'Thanks, Lily. I'd never have managed the zip on my own.'

Lily's eyes glowed with warmth. 'You look beautiful and...*happy*.' The sky-blue silk of her dress rustled as she walked to the door. 'I'd better get back to Rosie; she's a bundle of nerves and she needs me. I'll see you later.'

She smiled and left the room, closing the door softly behind her.

The cream-and-pale-green shoes stood to attention, ready for her to slip on, but instead Milla gazed at her reflection in the tall mirror.

After everything that had happened she could hardly believe that she was standing here, dressing for Rosie's wedding.

The dramas of last night seemed unimportant now. Cormac had been right to take them away this morning—spending time together in the wilderness had glued them back together. Their kisses at the ancient bothy had healed her heart and restored her faith.

She smiled softly at the memory of his lips on hers, the coaxing warmth of his mouth, that sensation of sublime acquiescence. It had felt like falling into a painting, being washed by hues of an indefinable colour. She was in love with Cormac Buchanan. She knew it in her bones the way she knew how to mix colours to capture exactly the right shade on canvas.

She slid her feet into the exquisite shoes and sprayed perfume on her neck and wrists. She was grateful that Rosie's make-up artist had been able to fit her in alongside the bridesmaids—the professional makeover had transformed her pale, tired-looking face to a picture of glowing health, so she felt ready to face the scrutiny she was bound to attract as Cormac's guest.

On the dressing table, nestled in tissue, was the wrist corsage Rosie had ordered especially for her. Another kindness. Shades of plum and pink to complement the *eau-de-nil* of her dress and shoes.

She slipped it on and took a deep breath. She was ready.

She couldn't stop the tears edging into her eyes as Rosie and Fraser exchanged their vows and slipped their rings over shaking fingers. Rosie was stunning in a cream silk dress of perfect simplicity, her long hair swept up into a dishevelled chignon, adorned with tiny rosebuds and pearls.

Milla glanced up at Cormac and found him watching her, a look of bemusement on his face. He squeezed her hand as she dabbed at her eyes and she knew what he was thinking. He was remembering her 'fuss and bother' speech in his grandfather's studio.

She smiled at the memory, at the way they'd been with each other back then.

As Rosie and Fraser walked past them down the aisle and they threw handfuls of confetti up into the air Milla was sure that there had never been such a beautiful bride as Rosie.

While Cormac stood for formal photographs with his family she took a drink and wandered among the guests, occasionally dangling at the edge of groups who were enjoying the sunshine, the champagne and a chance to catch up with old friends. She didn't mind hovering on the fringes because she didn't want to talk to anyone. The only person she wanted to be with was Cormac.

And then he was there, striding towards her over the lawn, handsome in his Lovat tweed jacket and a kilt of muted oranges, blues and greens: the Buchanan antique tartan.

'Rosie wants you to come for a photo.'

'Really—why?'

He kissed her swiftly, slid an arm around her waist and propelled her towards the terrace. 'You know why.'

'I don't. I mean, we're not exactly a fixture...'

The words sounded clumsy and she lowered her eyes in embarrassment—she should have kept her mouth shut.

He stopped walking and gazed at her. 'Not yet, but we're a work in a progress, aren't we?' He smiled softly. 'Don't analyse it, okay? Just come for the photo because it's the last one, and the sooner we get it done, the sooner we can spend time together.'

Under the shade of a gazebo a string quartet was working its way through *The Four Seasons* whilst waiters topped up glasses and handed round dainty canapés. The awkward moment about the photograph passed into history as the afternoon slipped by in a happy haze of chatter.

Cormac introduced Milla to Emma, who embraced her warmly and showed a keen interest in her painting, being a graphic artist herself. Further introductions followed, until Milla's head was spinning with names and faces. She was glad when the piper, resplendent in full Highland dress, piped them into the elegant marquee for the wedding breakfast.

She cheered and clapped through the speeches, marvelled at the exquisite wedding cake—six tiers, each a different flavour—as well as the towering stack of cheeses, decorated with a cascade of glowing fruit. Everything was beautiful, and the sheer scale of this celebration was as far from Milla's own wedding dreams as it would be possible to go.

After Rosie and Fraser had entertained their guests with a choreographed first dance the *ceilidh* band struck up for the Gay Gordons. Cormac tugged her onto the dance floor, and as they spun round and round his wide smile and shining eyes reminded her of the young soldier he'd been in that photograph in his grandfather's studio.

When the band announced that the next dance would be Strip the Willow, he shrugged out of his jacket and loosened his tie, pulling her close so he could shout in her ear. 'Take off your shoes or you'll twist your ankle again!'

The pace was lively, and the force of the spins so powerful that after the dance they tumbled out of the marquee, breathless and dizzy. Outside, the light was almost gone, but a million tiny lights twinkled in the trees.

Cormac motioned upwards and laughed. 'You're looking at a day's work right there. I don't want to see another string of lights for as long as I live.'

'It's stunning. Overwhelming. The whole wedding has been magical—so big…larger than life.'

He threw an arm around her shoulders. 'Rosie knows how to put on a show, that's for sure. Let's go for a walk.'

She looked down at her feet. 'I'm not wearing any shoes.'

He pressed his lips together and sighed. 'Oh, well. I've done it before, I can do it again—'

'No, Cormac, you're not going to—' But she was already up in his arms, laughing into his neck. 'Where are we going?'

'Somewhere quiet.'

She wrapped her arms around him, felt the heat of his body pulsing through the sheer fabric of her dress. He walked away from the noise and the lights, carrying her through the last throes of nightfall onto the jetty. A pale moon reflected off the water, and as he set her down she noticed the bright pinprick of Venus, already shimmering in the sky.

She slipped her hands into his. 'When I walked off this jetty last night I thought I'd lost you.'

She felt his lips in her hair.

'I know you did. But you should have known better. I told you before—I can't keep you at arm's length.' He released her and scuffed the boards with his shoe. 'This jetty has witnessed many an adventure over the years.'

She looked over the edge at the dark, shifting water. 'I'll bet you've pushed plenty of people off here in your time.'

He laughed. 'Yes, so don't tempt me.'

She stepped away from him. 'You wouldn't… It's Rosie's dress—she'd never forgive you.'

He shook his head slowly and stepped towards her. 'No. I didn't bring you here to throw you into the loch.'

The intensity of his gaze was making her nervous. 'So, why did you bring me here?'

He placed his hands on her waist. 'I wanted to tell you how incredibly beautiful you are.'

She blushed. 'I had a very good make-up artist—'

He placed a finger on her lips. 'Shh. I'm not talking about make-up. You have a lovely face. What I'm trying to say is that you *are* beautiful. On the inside. You brought me back to life and now my head's spinning with possibilities.' He reached for her hands. 'What you said today, about us not being a permanent fixture—we need to talk about that.'

'Oh, no! I wasn't—I didn't mean anything by it. What I'm trying to say, rather badly, is that I wasn't angling—'

He laughed. 'I know you weren't—and don't worry, I'm not about to ask for your hand—but…'

She sighed with relief. She was in love with him, but she wouldn't have known what to do if he'd dropped to his knee on the jetty.

'I *do* have a proposal for you.' He smiled. 'Will you hear me out?'

She nodded.

He released her hands and walked to the end of the jetty. 'All week my father's been trying to persuade me to leave the Army and take over the estate, and I turned him down repeatedly because it felt like he was offering me a hiding place, somewhere to run away from my failure. I could never accept his offer on those terms.'

He turned around and looked into her face.

'But in the middle of the night I had an idea for the estate—a plan for diversification—and I'm hoping it might interest you.'

'Me? I don't know anything about Highland estates—'

'But you know about art.'

'What's that got to do with anything?'

'Come here.'

She walked to his side and he wrapped his arms around her shoulders, turning her to face the loch. 'You love all this, don't you? This place. I've seen it in your work.'

She slid her hands to his forearms, savoured the warmth of his skin beneath her fingers. 'Yes. Of course.'

She felt his cheeks lifting into a smile. 'I took you out this morning because I wanted to see your reaction to other parts of the estate—from an artist's point of view. I wanted a professional, unbiased opinion about what we could offer.'

She twisted round to look at him. 'What do you mean—what you could offer?'

'I want to build more bothies for artists on the estate; I want to share this place with people who love it.' He released her and turned her round to face him. 'We could run courses, workshops… There are more buildings close to the house—they could be converted into studio space and you could take artists into the hills on painting safaris. Everything we've done this week. I discussed it with my father before the wedding and he's ready to listen, but it won't work without you, Milla. You're the inspiration.'

His enthusiasm was infectious, and the idea was certainly appealing. Calcarron Estate would be the perfect artist's retreat. It had everything. Breathtaking landscapes on the doorstep, an established reputation with its existing bothy, not to mention an extremely attractive and capable Laird.

'So you're proposing…what? A business partnership?'

He shook his head and the look in his eyes caused her heart to beat a little faster.

He reached a hand to her face and smiled softly. 'I love you, and I can't imagine any kind of future without you in it, so what I'm actually proposing is…'

She felt her hand fly to her mouth as he dropped to one knee and pulled a small black box from his sporran.

He looked up and held her in his gaze. 'Will you marry me, Milla O'Brien?'

For a moment she couldn't speak, and then she was smiling and crying at the same time. 'I will… I absolutely will… But you said you weren't going to ask—'

He rose to his feet, his smile even wider than his smile in that photograph. 'I said I wasn't going ask for your hand—but that's because I want all of you, not just a hand.' He opened the ring box. 'This was my grandmother's ring…'

Milla stared at the solitaire diamond glittering against the dark velvet. 'It's beautiful.'

He pushed the ring onto her finger and pulled her into his arms. 'You're mine now, and I'm yours…always.'

As his lips found hers she couldn't imagine a more perfect moment, and then suddenly he released her.

'Look!'

She followed his gaze upwards and laughed in delight. Shimmering green curtains were dancing across the sky above them. 'Do you think the cosmos is trying to tell us something?'

He wrapped his arms around her and kissed her hair. 'Maybe, but it can't tell us anything we don't already know.'

* * * * *